ALEX MILWAY was born in 1978 in Hereford. After finishing art school and spending a number of years in magazine publishing, he finally managed to finish a book, *The Mousehunter*. *The Curse of Mousebeard* is his second novel. He lives in Crystal Palace with his girlfriend and a curly-haired cat called Milo.

www.themousehunter.com

*Also by Alex Milway*

# The Mousehunter

# The Mousehunter
## THE CURSE OF MOUSEBEARD

Written and Illustrated by
ALEX MILWAY

LITTLE, BROWN AND COMPANY
New York Boston

# For Maya

Little, Brown and Company

Hachette Book Group
237 Park Avenue, New York, NY 10017
Visit our website at www.lb-kids.com

Little, Brown and Company is a division of Hachette Book Group, Inc.
The Little, Brown name and logo are trademarks of Hachette Book Group, Inc.

First Edition: April 2010
First published in Great Britain in 2008 by Faber and Faber Limited

ISBN 978-0-316-07744-6

10 9 8 7 6 5 4 3 2 1

RRD-C

Printed in the United States of America

Mice may not rule the world, but
they have the power to shape it

from *The Ways and Means of Mice*,
Professor Rudolph Lugwidge

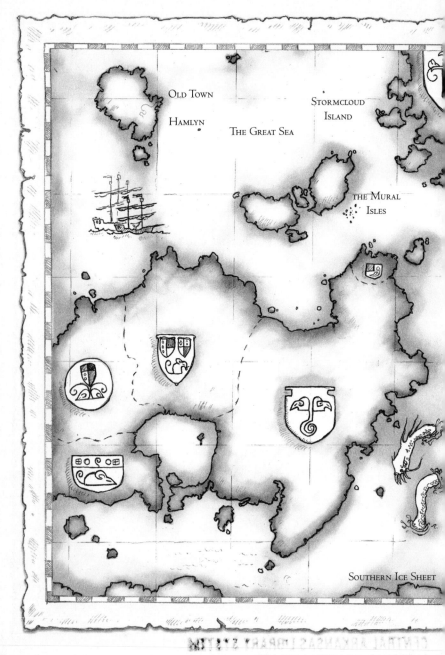

OLD TOWN

HAMLYN

THE GREAT SEA

STORMCLOUD
ISLAND

THE MURAL
ISLES

SOUTHERN ICE SHEET

DRAGON
NSULAR

THE EASTERN SEA

N

THE BARREN SEA

The Southern Seas
for Mousehunters

Here be
Monsters

Emiline

Miserley

Scratcher

Drewshank

Indigo

Algernon

Mousebeard

Battersby

# Goodbye to Old Town

HORATIO SPIRES RETREATED INTO THE HALLWAY NEXT TO Lovelock's office and scribbled on a piece of paper. He acted swiftly, his ears alert to the muffled words escaping from next door.

"I shall set sail as soon as we have a favorable wind," said Lord Battersby.

Spires heard his master laugh triumphantly, and the door clicked as it started to unlock. A bead of sweat trickled down the butler's forehead, and with a final press of his pen against the paper in his hand, he stood upright and slid the note into his suit pocket.

"There's no immediate rush, Alexander," said Lovelock.

"I can assure you, our friend Mousebeard will know nothing of this."

"Even so, I'm quite in the mood for a spot of exploration. The *Stonebreaker* only grows barnacles in port—she'd be much happier at sea!"

"Well, don't let me stop you," added Lovelock. "The Golden Mice may well look like pennies next to the treasures out there. You must thank your codebreakers for me!"

The door opened fully, and Spires righted his glasses as the dull grey light of morning crept into the hallway.

"I assure you I will," said Battersby cheerfully, "and I promise to send word of any discoveries as soon as we're within messaging range."

As Battersby left the room, he looked to the butler and his expression changed to one of seriousness. Their eyes met, and an icy chill seeped into Spires's heart.

"Good day, sir," said Spires, a slight fragility to his voice.

Battersby snorted, pulled his collar high, and marched down the stairs, letting his boots clomp loudly. Spires knew of Lord Battersby's moods, but there was more to that look than mere grumpiness. Taking a long, deep breath, he walked to Lovelock's office and knocked on the door before entering. Rain was rattling the window behind Lovelock, and a distant growl of thunder rumbled aloud. Spires stood upright.

"Will that be all for the moment, sir?" he asked calmly.

"That's all, thank you," replied Lovelock, a smile still apparent on his face.

"Very good, sir," said Spires.

# The Silver Shark

# Algernon's Submarine

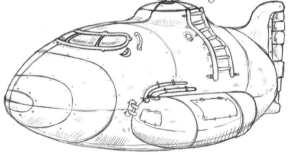

# The Tour Guide and the Teacher

"Now then," said the delighted tour guide as she skipped down to the gun deck, her tightly bunched hair moving not an inch, "the *Silver Shark* was an immensely powerful warship in its time. Here, for example, you'll see the deadly cannons. These weapons are said to have killed six thousand men at the least!"

The group of ten children and their schoolmaster all cooed in awe. They were a visiting party from the land of Tamaroy and, as well as the customary mouseboxes that hung from their belts, they were dressed in its traditional dress of red cape, puffy trousers, and floppy black hats.

"But maybe of more interest to you aspiring young mousekeepers, if you listen very hard, below your feet you'll hear the scurrying of a very interesting species of mouse."

Everyone fell silent. A few of the children crouched to the floor and pressed their ears to the boards.

"It would seem that Mousebeard had a love of Mustachioed Mice," added the guide, "as there is a very large family of them living between the planks on this lower deck. We have a small band that comes and plays here each evening to keep them happy. They do miss the regular shanties of the pirates, unfortunately, but we do what we can."

"Mustachioed Mice?" queried one of the children. "Mousebeard the pirate liked those wussy mice?"

"Ah, yes," said the guide. "There are many peculiar things now coming to light about the notorious pirate. I bet you didn't know that he liked Andamam Cheese, for a start?"

"The one with all the pickled mouse droppings in it?" exclaimed the schoolmaster.

"The one and only! We found three truckles of the stuff in the pantry."

"Urgh!" exclaimed the children in unison.

"And along with those we found fifty-three skewered Bonbon Mice, each sugared in a fine pink coating. He obviously had a very fine taste in delicacies!"

"So Mousebeard may have been barbarous and evil, but he did have a fine palate. Education gets you a long way, see!" said the schoolmaster to his pupils.

"Trained at the Old Rodents' Academy, no less!" added the guide.

"And that's where all the cleverest and hardest-working students end up," added the schoolmaster. "They often take foreign mousekeeping students, so there's every chance you could all win a scholarship!"

He then walked up to the tour guide and whispered a few words.

"Yes, you're right!" said the guide, gesturing to the children. "There is a brig downstairs in the hull—the darkest and scariest place on all the ship!"

The mousekeepers chattered nervously to one another, their hats flapping at their heads.

"Would you like to see it?" she said excitedly.

"Yeeeessss!" they all shouted.

"Right then, this way!"

The tour guide bounced down the stairs and lit the few oil lamps around the walls.

"This is where all the prisoners were kept!" said the guide as the children filtered down the stairs, followed by their master. The young mousekeepers were clearly in awe.

"Who wants to see what it's like to be locked in Mousebeard's brig?" said the schoolmaster.

The tour guide looked a bit uneasy.

"That's quite unusual, Mr. Sparks; we don't generally allow such things."

"Oh, but us Tamarovians believe it's good for the children to experience everything. It's all part of learning and growing up!" said the teacher, standing more upright and scratching his scruffy beard.

After a short consultation with her notes, the guide agreed and walked to the iron bars that sealed off the prison in the tip of the bow.

"Come on then, children, in you come!"

The guide pulled on the chains, and the bars lifted to the ceiling.

Once all the children had entered the brig, the school-master walked to the tour guide.

"It must have been horrible to have been locked in there," he said gloomily, the lamplight flickering off his round glasses.

"Most definitely!" she replied.

"Say, why don't we lower the bars again, just for a moment, to see what it's like?" said the schoolmaster.

"Oh, I don't know…"

"What harm could it do?"

"Are you all right with this, children?" she asked.

"Yeeesss!" they replied excitedly.

"Well, all right then…"

She reached up for the chain and pulled hard. There was a noisy, rusty squeal, and just as the bars started to tilt and lower, three of the children dashed out and pulled firmly at her skirt. Her legs twisted beneath her and she tumbled forward. All the other mousekeepers jumped on her, muffling her screams, and within seconds she was bound and gagged.

"Ready?" asked the schoolmaster, removing Tamaroy's national dress to reveal the clothes of a ship's captain.

"As ever…," announced Emiline, removing her hat and cape as she strolled from the brig.

"You were great, sir!" cheered Scratcher, swinging his mousebox around his waist and removing his cape. "They had no idea!"

"I'd always fancied myself as an actor," he replied, swishing his hair back and tearing the fake beard from his face.

The rest of the young mousekeepers laughed and walked out of the brig, leaving the tour guide to wriggle helplessly. Drewshank pulled the chain, and the iron bars swung down to seal the brig.

"You were all brilliant!" said Emiline enthusiastically. Her Grey Mouse, Portly, appeared on her shoulder and gave a triumphant squeak. "But now we've got to get this ship ready to move."

She flipped open her pocket watch and checked the time.

"We've got to hurry," she added, turning to the trusty mousekeepers. "You guys, you know what to do. If you've got Rigger Mice in your boxes, release them on the top deck, get them up to speed, and secure the rigging for the sails. The rest of you, close off the gun deck so there's no open gun holes, then release your Wailer Mice. Once you've done that, climb the masts and get ready for our commands. Scratcher, you find Mousebeard's secret stash of weapons. I hope he's right in thinking they'll still be here...."

⇒ ✳ ⇐

Algernon made slow, plodding steps along the seabed in his metal underwater suit—each step taking twice as much effort as usual. Fish buzzed about in front of him, attracted by the bright blue lights beaming from the glass eyeholes. One of the suit's robotic arms lifted to his eye line, and he noted the time displayed on its dimly lit dial.

"Come on, Algernon," he muttered to himself, his breath spreading condensation inside the helmet. "Five minutes! Five minutes!"

He looked around, focusing the lights on the hulls of ships below the waterline as he trudged along. Mousebeard's ship was impounded at the far end of the harbor, and just as a spiky eel whizzed past, the lights reflected off the makeshift wall that trapped it in Old Town. Built of huge boulders, the wall was held in place by a mesh of thick iron poles. Algernon twisted a valve to release some extra hydraulic power, and immediately his legs were able to move faster along the sandy floor until he finally reached its base.

He trailed the lights from his helmet upward and saw the shiny metal hull of the *Silver Shark* breaking cleanly out of the water. It was raining heavily, and the water's surface looked as though it was being hit by thousands of tiny meteorites.

"No time to lose!" he muttered. Inside his suit, his hands twisted a few levers, and with a whizz and a shudder, his second robotic arm extended outward, and a thick drill started to whirr at its end. It vibrated heavily as it bored deep into the side of a boulder, sending a cloud of dirt gushing into the water. Algernon held it steady for a few seconds, then flicked a switch and the drill slowed to a stop before shrinking back into the arm. A claw flicked out to take its place, which then swung around to the suit's back, unhinged a thin cylinder, and pushed it into the drill-hole.

Algernon felt sweat trickle down his forehead. He lifted the second robotic arm and checked the time again.

"Thirty seconds!" he said hurriedly. "Oh my! Almost ready…"

The claw twisted the cylinder's end, upon which a red light started to flash. Algernon hurriedly secured the two robotic arms and turned the suit around. With the press of a button and the release of another valve inside, a gush of air burst out from the suit's back. His body lifted from the seabed, and he shot off at hair-raising speed.

⇒ ✳ ⇐

Emiline and Drewshank reached the top deck and walked out into the pouring rain. The deck was empty but for a lone guard at the gangplank that led down onto the quayside. Ever since the *Silver Shark* had been securely impounded, the Old Town Guard had seen little point in keeping watch over the ship.

Drewshank and Emiline crept around the deck until they were just a few meters from the soldier.

"Where's Spires?" whispered Emiline, as rain dripped from her nose. "He was supposed to be here?"

"He should have been, but we can't worry about it,"

Drewshank said. "Spires will have to make his own escape. How long do we have?"

"We can't go without him!" she pleaded.

"We must...," he added firmly. "Now, how long do we have?"

Emiline looked at her pocket watch.

"Hold on tight! Four...three...two...one..."

An immense underwater explosion kicked the ship into the air and blasted huge rocks and debris onto the quayside. The ship fell back onto the sea—lifting water far over the quayside in a great wave. Drewshank jumped out and hit the soldier over the head before knocking him into the water. Emiline rushed after him, grabbed the gangplank, and pulled it in desperately. She looked up to see soldiers and sailors charging onto the quay from the taverns and stores.

"We're in for it now!" said Drewshank.

"Emiline!" shouted Scratcher, sliding a sword along the deck for her. "He certainly wasn't lying! More swords than I could carry!"

Emiline continued to haul in the gangplank with Drewshank's help. Its farthest end reared up and eventually clicked into place, and once again the *Silver Shark*'s deck was fully protected by its tall armored sides.

"Get the sails open!" shouted Drewshank to all the mousekeepers up in the rigging. The children began frantically pulling at the sail tethers, and the Rigger Mice scurried back and forth, helping them by biting through knots.

"Where are the Wailer Mice?" called Drewshank.

"In position!" replied Scratcher, trying to get his bearings. He'd been on the *Silver Shark* only briefly in the past, and it wasn't the fondest of memories, but he was getting a feel for it now. The sails on the mainmast tumbled down and immediately caught the wind. The ship nudged forward just as three grappling hooks shot over the side and caught firm. Its escape was halted.

"Captain Drewshank!" shouted Emiline, running to the ship's wheel. "They're trying to get on board!"

The sound of gunfire filled the air. Scratcher responded by pulling clods of wool from his pocket and handing them to Emiline and Drewshank.

"Stick them in your ears!" he said, before placing two fingers in his mouth. He gave a high-pitched whistle, and the Wailer Mice immediately started wailing from the mainmast. It was absolutely deafening, and everyone on the quayside clamped their hands to their ears.

"Get the other sails down!" ordered Drewshank, although no one could hear him. He threw off the grappling hooks, cast them into the water, and started swinging his arms to catch everyone's attention; but his lightweight crew already had the task in hand.

The mousekeepers now worked faster than ever before. Their small hands made a swift job of untying all the knots. Finally, the second sail dropped, and the wind caught it fully.

"Captain Drewshank!" called Emiline, waving frantically. "A gunship!"

The ship's wheel was raised slightly, allowing the pilot to see above the armored hull. Emiline had seen that just a short distance away, a huge warship was turning out from its berth. Drewshank saw her calling.

"They're getting ready to fire!" she shouted. Drewshank gripped his forehead in frustration. They weren't getting anywhere fast. The *Silver Shark* creaked as it drifted forward and slowly worked its way out through the demolished wall. A loud broadside blew out of the gunship, sending clouds of smoke into the air. Two cannonballs shot straight through the *Silver Shark*'s sails and flew into houses around the edges of the docks. Numerous cries called out from the quayside in terror.

"Come on!" shouted Scratcher, now at Emiline's side. "We're not going anywhere!"

"We'll get there," replied Emiline hoarsely, as another hail of cannon fire hit the side of the ship, sending shockwaves along its deck. The *Silver Shark*'s armor held firm, and gradually the vessel built up speed as it moved farther and farther away from the quayside. The only harbor exit was a narrow break in the thick seawall. There was no room for mistakes.

"I thought this ship was supposed to be fast?" muttered Drewshank, rushing to the bow. He stepped up a short ladder and peered through the rain at the gunship, now fully on the move toward them.

"They're after us!" he shouted. Drewshank looked to the harbor and saw crowds of people bustling around. A battalion of soldiers, lined up along the seawall, lifted their rifles to fire, and Drewshank hurled himself at the deck.

"We've got to get out of here!" he shouted, banging his hand on the floor.

Scratcher rushed to his side to see if he was all right.

"What did you say?" he shouted.

"Lose that ship!"

"Oh!" said Scratcher.

"And shut those mice up..."

Scratcher whistled loudly, and the ear-piercing wail squeaked to a halt.

"Thank you!"

"Any time."

"They're catching us!" shouted a young mousekeeper from up on the second mast.

Above the *Silver Shark*'s armored side, Emiline watched the sails of the gunship in the distance. Drewshank stood up and rushed to her side.

"Not far now," she said through gritted teeth. She had to navigate into a route only eighty meters wide at the most: the open sea was nearing and her hands gripped the wheel tighter. The ship fired at them once more, and cannonballs splashed down into the water just ahead of them.

"Keep her steady!" said Drewshank. More shots whizzed overhead.

"How are we going to escape them?" asked Emiline, catching sight of the gunship over her shoulder.

"Don't worry," said Drewshank, pulling his collar tight to stop the rain from getting in. "Our man Algernon has that sorted...I hope."

Emiline managed a smile. The *Silver Shark* was getting harder to control, but that meant only one thing: it was picking up speed, and in seconds the huge, algae-covered seawalls were on either side of them.

"Come on, Algernon," said Drewshank. He started tapping his hands against his legs, sensing the gunship was nearing. Its cannons fired again, and they hit the rear of the *Silver Shark* full-on. The hull pitched forward slightly with the impact, but Emiline maintained her footing and the ship's course.

Scratcher ran along the deck to the rear of the ship. He swung open the door into Mousebeard's cabin and rushed to look out of the small rounded window at the back. The gunship was closing in. It was easily the equal of the *Silver Shark* and had four front-mounted cannons trained — it seemed — on him. They fired again. Scratcher dropped to the floor and heard a colossal explosion as the *Silver Shark* took the hit.

"But cannonballs don't explode?" he said.

Scratcher jumped to his feet and looked out the window. The gunship was on fire, with a blossoming column of smoke rising from its deck. The two walls on either side of it that heralded the calm of Old Town's harbor were in tatters, and huge rocks lay strewn everywhere.

"Algernon, you did it!" he laughed.

Scratcher ran back onto the deck and found Drewshank and Emiline with smiles on their faces.

"We did it!" said Drewshank proudly.

"Proper fugitives now…," added Emiline. "We'll be as wanted as Mousebeard!"

"With our own posters!" cheered Scratcher. He looked up and called to all the mousekeepers to come down onto the deck. They were drenched, but overjoyed at having taken part in such an exciting event.

As the rain grew heavier, the *Silver Shark* powered through the waves like a silver bullet. With Emiline at the helm and its very small crew rushing back and forth, its course was set: the Isle of Glum awaited them.

⇒ ✳ ⇐

Spires ran toward the quayside, but he was too late. Soldiers were everywhere, and the sound of gunfire filled the air as the *Silver Shark* drifted away. He pulled his hood down further to shield his eyes, and waited silently.

"What would Mousebeard do?" he thought to himself, as cannonballs smashed into the buildings behind him. It had been years since he'd seen a battle, and he felt his confidence growing. Ever since he had taken part in rescuing Mousebeard, his hunger for adventure had slowly replaced his fear.

The butler looked around at the harbor: there were fishing vessels aplenty, as well as the countless naval ships that now littered the port. Even with all the drama surrounding him, there had to be some way of securing passage out of Old Town. He felt the thick wad of schillings inside his pocket and remembered something his friend Algernon used to say: "A sailor charmed is only half as willing as a sailor paid."

He smiled to himself and started searching for a captain who looked down on his luck.

# The Wailer Mouse

THIS PECULIARLY UGLY MOUSE IS KNOWN FOR ITS EAR-PIERCING SHRIEK, THE *sound of which can travel for miles across water and, at worst, can deafen a human. In order to create such a din, the mouse inflates a large air sac in its throat and then forces the air out through its teeth like a whistle.*

*The Wailer Mouse was first discovered only forty-two years ago on a small island called Erta on the edge of the Great Sea. A group of the mice were found clustered on a craggy clifftop above what could only be described as a ship graveyard. It is now thought that the ships' sailors fell victim to the collected noise of the mice and lost their minds and bearings.*

### MOUSING NOTES

*Due to its aggressive shrieking, and the problems this could cause within a town environment, the Wailer Mouse is a banned species.*

# The Pirate Mousehunting Club

THE ISLE OF GLUM SAT ALONE IN A VAST BROODING SEA, with nothing but choppy waves and the occasional lost Stubby-nosed Seal Mouse for company. It wasn't quite bare—a lone wilting pine tree stood upon its grey stone back—but there was nothing of any worth for a tourist to visit. If you had a keen interest in mice and were a pirate, however, this was one of the most talked-about places in the world.

Accessible only from the water, and then visible only if you navigated past a field of razor-sharp rocks standing proudly out of the sea, a wide cave cut deep into Glum. Its course twisted far into the island's stomach like a saltwater sewer, bringing all manner of dirty, stinking, mouse-fixated pirates deep underground.

For way below Glum's surface, the long, twisting cave eventually opened out into a glistening cavern the size of six cathedrals at the least. A serene lake filled its bottom, and around its edges were all manner of seafaring vessels resting peacefully. Buildings were hewn into the rock face or clung to the ceiling like Cave Mouse dung, with solid wooden tendrils descending into the lake to hold them up. A series of walkways crisscrossed the space like a giant cobweb, and torches flickered restlessly every few meters along their sides.

Pirates could be seen everywhere, huddled in discussion or caught up in heated debate about rodents. And if ever there was a place where pirates could be seen as being civilized, it was Glum.

The Pirate Mousehunting Club that ran the facilities on the island demanded only one thing: that the island should remain a secret, even on pain of death. Pirates rarely play by the rules, but as testament to how important the island was, only one known man had ever foolishly let slip the location. His name was Big Bones Alkin, and both he and his unfortunate confidants came to a swift and untimely death when they were forcibly chained to an iron post on Luckgone Island—hunting ground of the deadly Slime-toothed Fang Mouse. It would have been a very messy end for any creature.

This rule meant that Glum provided the most perfect hiding place for people wanting to stay out of the authorities' way. And for Mousebeard, this was exactly what was required.

The pirate rested in a wooden cabin at the uppermost point of the cave. It was bolted to the cavern rock face with immense iron screws, and the floorboards creaked ominously with every movement. Mousebeard sat quietly at a table lit by candlelight, with a huge map spread out wide before him. He teased his beard between his fingers, occasionally scratching the backs of the few mice that he'd borrowed from fellow pirates and placed within. They didn't make up for his own mice that had been stolen and now resided in Isiah Lovelock's collection, but they would do.

His dark eyes stared at an island—a long way from Glum—that was drawn with clouds all around its edges. Small words were scribbled over it: "Stormcloud Island—land at your peril."

Mousebeard rapped his fingers on the table.

"What's your problem?" said Fenwick, resting against the wall. His rough sailor's hands rubbed over his shaved head. "They'll get your blasted ship back!"

The pirate turned and glowered at the man, the candles picking up the shiny eyes of the mice in his beard.

"I'm worried," he said. "It's been over a week."

"They don't need your cares," replied Fenwick angrily. "You're only interested in your ship and your curse, no matter what you say."

"Fenwick...," the pirate growled, but stopped his words short. Someone had knocked at the thin door. "Come in!"

"It's Ingrid," announced a scratchy but friendly voice. The door swung open.

"Your ship's arrived," said Ingrid Hoodwink, an aging pirate with puffed-up trousers and wild straw-colored hair. Behind her stood Chervil, the onetime ship's cat of the *Flying Fox*. Ever since being brought to Glum it had never left her side; wisely, since most mousecollectors hated cats more than anything. No one dared touch it, though, as Ingrid had been a resident at Glum for nearly thirty years and was the closest anyone got to being in charge of the place.

"They made it?" cheered Fenwick, rushing headfirst through the door, his mouse clinging to his shirt collar for dear life.

"It's causing quite a stir among the newest residents," she said.

"Ah...your hospitality has proved limitless, Ingrid," said Mousebeard, folding up his map and rising to his feet. He picked his mouse-bitten tricorn hat from the table and pulled it tightly onto his head.

"If there's ever a way to repay your kindness, you only have to ask."

Ingrid blushed slightly. In the world of pirates, Mousebeard was a celebrity held in great respect, but among the mouse-keeping ranks he was as close to a living god as you could get—especially after his recent escape from the gallows.

"Thank you, sir," she said joyously, and skipped out of the cabin with wind in her sails. Before she had gotten too far away, however, she stopped and delved into her trouser pocket.

"Oh, sir," she added seriously, pulling out a small clipping from the *Mousing Times*. "I saw this....Please be careful!"

She passed it to the pirate, and he stared at the headline, nothing more. "Illyrian Death Squads seek vengeance for Golden Mice," it read.

"Thank you again, Ingrid," he said. "I promise I won't let any near me."

Mousebeard stepped onto the ropewalk that ran from his door to a rickety staircase along the cave wall. He gripped the firm handrail and peered over to see the lake way down below. There was his ship, the *Silver Shark*, shimmering in the flickering light as though cut from the purest diamond. A group of pirates had huddled at its side, and despite a few battle scars and war wounds here and there, it looked in fine fettle.

He walked the long route down to the lake with many eyes upon him. Mousebeard had hardly left his cabin since his arrival on Glum for fear of arousing too much interest, and with the bounty on his head doubled since his escape from Old Town he was still wary of any loose talk. He checked the swords at his side and pulled the buckles at his waist to ensure they were secure.

"Drewshank!" he shouted, dropping the final few steps onto one of the floating pontoons that rested across the lake as makeshift docks.

A gangplank clunked down from the side of the *Silver Shark*, and Devlin Drewshank marched forth. He shook Fenwick's hand, resisting a manly hug from his stocky first mate, but he was happy to see his friend nonetheless. Then he saw the shape of Mousebeard in the distance.

"I told you we'd make it," Drewshank said aloud, navigating the crowd like a true celebrity in order to reach the pirate. "Look, not a scratch on her!"

Mousebeard's beard bulged out sideways, as what could only be described as a smile formed on his usually stern face.

"You didn't let me down," he said. "That's twice I owe you now.... And everyone else?"

The young mousekeepers ran down the gangplank and were immediately swamped by the crowd — consisting mainly of their pirate parents. Emiline and Scratcher followed and were quickly grasped between the arms of Fenwick, who was overjoyed to see them.

"And Algernon? Horatio?" asked Mousebeard.

"I'm here!" called Algernon, skipping down the gangplank. His submarine sat on the top deck, lashed down by iron chains and ropes. He'd spent most of the journey on board resting in one of the ship's hammocks.

"Spires wasn't there to meet us," said Drewshank, his tone serious.

"He wasn't? But we've received no word from him...," said Mousebeard.

"No, nor us," added Algernon. "But Horatio is a man of many talents and resources. Let's give him a few weeks, and if we've still heard nothing, then we should act."

Mousebeard nodded, patted his wide hand on Algernon's shoulder, and started to walk toward his ship.

"Oh, and we've managed to find ourselves a prisoner...," said Drewshank sheepishly. "She's held in the brig...."

"A prisoner? That doesn't sound like the actions of Captain Drewshank," said Mousebeard, laughing.

"She seems very nice... and peculiarly, she seemed overjoyed by the whole experience."

Mousebeard put his arm around Drewshank and whispered quietly in his ear.

"You'd better not let anyone here know about her. They don't take kindly to outsiders," he said, smiling.

"Oh I wouldn't dream of it," replied Drewshank. "But she has mentioned how much she'd like to meet you...."

Mousebeard's eyes grew dark and menacing.

"What have you told her about me?"

Drewshank could feel fear welling in his belly.

"She was the tour guide on the *Shark*," he replied nervously. "I think she knows more about you and your ship than even yourself."

Mousebeard's face broke and he laughed louder than he had in years.

"I'd better make her feel welcome then," he said, "before casting her adrift on the stormiest sea I can find!"

Drewshank had no idea whether the pirate was joking or not, and he made a valiant attempt at a smile.

"Get us food and drink!" shouted Mousebeard, lifting his arms in the air. He walked past the menacing shark's teeth painted on the hull of his ship and realized he was soon to be free again.

"Tomorrow brings us a new adventure, but tonight we shall feast!"

⇒ ✳ ⇐

"They've left it clean and tidy at least," grumbled Mouse-beard, as he tore into a thick joint of meat. Three tables were lined up along the gun deck, all covered in food fit for a queen. Overflowing jars of Honey Mouse Ale rested by everyone's plates, as well as an array of assorted sweetmeats provided by Ingrid Hoodwink herself.

"But the mist generator's gone," said Algernon, "as are the front cannons. I imagine they're making use of them—it's not like the Old Town Guard to miss an opportunity like that."

"Hmph. Typical of Isiah to take what's not his…"

Drewshank was listening to their conversation, and he felt like speaking.

"Isiah Lovelock again…," he said, quaffing some ale. "Are we always going to be bothered by him?"

Mousebeard stuck a dirty fingernail between two of his teeth and dug out a piece of gristle. He chewed it once more, then swallowed it down.

"Our paths will always cross," said the pirate. "But until I've put an end to this blasted curse that stops me setting foot on land, I can never finish him. And I intend to—take my word for it—with my own bare hands."

"So you're determined to find a means of breaking the curse?" said Algernon.

"We leave tomorrow for Stormcloud Island..."

Algernon shook his head.

"You know full well what occurred last time you visited that place—and you still don't care to tell me what truly happened," he said.

Mousebeard growled, and realized that the time had come to explain all.

"The curse...," he said gruffly.

Suddenly, all fell silent, as though the very word drew their attention away from what they were doing. Emiline and Scratcher turned to the pirate, as did Fenwick and the other sailors who surrounded the table.

"I suppose you all should hear...," he said reluctantly, seeing everyone's eyes stare at his. "The curse took control of Isiah and me on a small outcrop in the Great Sea called Stormcloud Island. It was our intention to find a woman there who owned a Methuselah Mouse — one of the rarest mice on the planet, with the supposed power to live for thousands of years. Isiah often said he would pay the woman well for this mouse, but we both thought it would be an honor just to see such a creature. At least that was what I thought.

"True to the island's name, when we landed, it was covered by the largest, most brooding black clouds you could imagine. The wind lashed waves into terrifying peaks and troughs around its rocky shores, and we left Algernon to keep hold of our sailboat at the broken wooden jetty — a wise choice, as I later found out. The rain fell so hard, but we rushed across the boulders, soon finding a path that led higher and higher until we were marching through the frothing clouds.

"Eventually we reached a stone building, smoke bursting its way out of the chimneys, and we knew we'd found what we were looking for. We banged on the door — it took ages for its occupant to answer, but she did. I believe the woman hadn't seen a human for years, so surprised was she to see us standing like bedraggled fancy mice on her doorstep. She was fairly old, and short, and her hair was sagging scruffily around her head. I remember her expression upon seeing us as if it were yesterday. She was wary, maybe even scared, but her eyes showed such interest in us. She finally invited us in — Isiah was always a charmer and could persuade almost anyone to do as he asked — and we were shown into a room. It was so lushly decorated inside: intricate tapestries hung from the walls provided warmth and color, and oil lamps glowed with that rare orange light only they can give.

"When Isiah first mentioned the mouse, she threatened to send us away; such was her feeling about it. But he managed to persuade her once more. In truth, I think she was pleased with the company, although as we soon found out, she was much more than she let on.

"When she revealed the Methuselah Mouse, I found it near impossible to restrain my excitement. I cannot explain how amazing it was — so old, so wrinkled and shriveled, and its eyes looked so dead — but when it's before you, it makes the hairs on the back of your neck stand on end. And that feeling was what turned Isiah. I'd seen the greed and lust in him before, but we were friends, and it had always been a joke among us that he would never be happy until he owned the world. But the Methuselah Mouse stirred something evil in him.

"He told the woman he wanted it and was willing to pay a small fortune for the honor of owning it. But she had no use for money and swiftly told us to leave. Of course, Isiah was unwilling to accept this. He argued with her and bullied her, trying everything to get her to part with it. All my efforts to calm him failed. I tried to hold him back, but he lunged at the woman in an attempt to snatch the mouse, his eyes crazed like a madman. And that was it. The last I remember was the crackling blue light and the deafening shriek that filled the room. My heart felt like it was being crushed with such an unimaginable pain; it was unbearable, like having your life—your very soul—squeezed out of you.

"When I awoke, I was outside. I couldn't breathe. Isiah stood staring at me, the rain streaming in rivers down his face. He looked gaunt and much older. I rose to my feet but found my chest twisting and shrinking—every breath shorter and shorter. I looked at Isiah through my blurring eyes. He wasn't in pain; he just watched me struggle. I tumbled and tripped, desperately trying to find my footing and the energy to reach Algernon. I still don't know how I managed to make my way to the boat, but I did. And at that point, as I fell into the hull, I suddenly felt the pain subside. It took a long time before I realized, with the help of Algernon, that I couldn't set foot on land. It is the most horrifying feeling of all, to have your life changed so fully, in such a swift, short moment, with no means of doing anything about it. The pain was so great, I deemed never to speak about what happened. But I feel things are different now. Matters are coming to a head, and I must face my demons once and for all.

"That she was a witch is beyond doubt, but there must be a way to counter the curse. There must be a way.... Which is why tomorrow we set sail for Stormcloud Island, with the intention of settling this issue."

"But who's going to want to land?" asked Algernon, finally understanding what had haunted Mousebeard for so long.

Drewshank started to shake his head as he saw everyone's eyes home in on him.

"Oh no...," he said, looking around the table. "Oh no, no, no..."

"You know how important this matter is, Drewshank," said Mousebeard. "This is the last time I will ask anything from you. I'm sure Emiline and Scratcher would relish the opportunity to go on a sort of mousehunt—you could lead the expedition."

"It sounds more like a witch hunt to me," snapped Drewshank, "and I have very little in the way of magic skills to protect me. No, hang on...oh yes, that's right, I have no abilities in the way of magic...."

"I don't believe in magic," said Algernon. "I think there's more here than witchcraft."

"Well, that sounds even better!" Drewshank replied sarcastically, appearing quite upset.

"But, Captain Drewshank," said Emiline, "who better to charm an old witch than yourself? I know you'd win her over in no time."

Everyone around the table made noises in agreement.

"You think?" he said, raising an eyebrow.

"Definitely!" said Scratcher.

"There's none better than you, Drewshank," said Mouse-beard. "Your charm might even rival that of Lovelock."

Drewshank needed no more praise; his mind was turned.

"Well, if you put it that way," he said, "what are we waiting for? Stormcloud Island, here we come…"

# The Slime-toothed Fang Mouse

FOUND ONLY ON LUCKGONE ISLAND—A DISUSED PIRATE OUTPOST IN THE *Great Sea* — *the Slime-toothed Fang Mouse is a vile creature. It is well known for its vicious tendencies and very sharp fangs, and it earns its name because it secretes a type of poisonous slime from its gums. This slime stops wounds from healing and blood from clotting, and so, for any victim, it ensures a fate worse than death.*

## MOUSING NOTES

*One bite from this creature means a slow, lingering death, and so it would make no sense to keep this in any collection.*

# Stormcloud Island

IT TOOK THREE WEEKS FOR THE SILVER SHARK TO REACH Stormcloud Island. A landing party was agreed upon, and while the ship dropped anchor farther out at sea to avoid damage, a small rowing boat struggled over the breaking waves with the wind and rain lashing around it. Scratcher was thoroughly dismayed at his own decision to travel with them. Water dribbled down through his hood, dripping time after time on the end of his nose. He clutched the rim of the boat, digging in his fingertips as Fenwick pulled the oars for one last time, bringing them into line with the shabby, broken jetty.

The island was immersed in weather. Rain fell in

torrents, wind blew haphazardly across its rocky surface, and clouds frothed over its highest peak.

"That'll be it then," said Fenwick, tossing a rope around a wooden plank and pulling it tight into him. "I'll be waiting here with the boat. You all take care of yourselves…."

"Thanks…," muttered Drewshank, trying to stand as the boat wobbled under his feet. "Mousebeard's onto a good thing here, I'm sure of it. Why did I agree to this? Him sending us all over the place while he gets to put his feet up…"

Emiline stood up and smiled, relishing the prospect of an adventure.

"You know he'd swap his position any day," she said, leaping to the few remaining wooden planks of the jetty that were joined to the rocks. Scratcher steadied himself and leapt after Emiline.

"Come on, Captain," he said, landing awkwardly with his hands on the floor. Emiline pulled him out of the way as Drewshank jumped across. He landed safely and flicked his jacket to shake off some rain.

"It's wet and disgusting," said Drewshank firmly. "Who in their right mind would come here?"

Emiline took no notice and made the first steps onto the large, slippery boulders that led to the island. The rain was swirling around, distorting and confusing the route ahead, and she had to be careful to dodge the Limpet Mice who lay all around. These oily, short-haired mice had evolved suckers on their paws that let them attach to rocks without a care for the elements or personal safety.

"Mousebeard said to walk inland until we found a path," she said, marching over the rugged terrain.

Scratcher pulled his hood down further and followed her footsteps precisely. She was rushing on at quite a pace, and even Drewshank was struggling to keep up.

"Here it is!" she shouted.

A narrow path was cut into the bedrock, winding upward, and a shimmering stream of water ran down it like a gutter heading out to sea. As soon as Emiline stepped into it, her boots became swamped with water.

"This way!" she shouted, trying to pay no attention to the slushing noise emanating from her feet.

The group continued upward, and the rain grew stronger to the point that it almost hurt their heads as they walked in it. Scratcher ran to reach Emiline, and he tapped her on the shoulder.

"We should be nearly there, Emiline," he said, wiping water from his forehead. "Mousebeard was certain we'd see it before too long."

Emiline nodded and waited for Drewshank to join them.

"I wasn't made for this sort of thing," said Drewshank grumpily. He looked at the mousekeepers, but his stare suddenly lifted to the horizon. Being that much taller than Emiline and Scratcher, he could see over the brow of the hill they were climbing.

"Well, I never. There it is!" he said.

Emiline and Scratcher sprinted up the last few meters of the path and eventually saw what he was talking about. Standing out from the doom-laden sky was a rectangular, rugged stone building with three wide chimneys breaking free of its roof. Its blackened, shadowy exterior made it look like the least friendly house in existence.

"Just as he described it!" said Scratcher. "The one place you'd not want to go for dinner…"

"Come on then," said Drewshank; "the sooner we find out what's going on in there, the sooner we can leave."

They hurried on and gradually the building revealed itself. Its aging stone facade showed no signs of life, with no light escaping from spaces in the shuttered windows. No smoke broke free of the chimneys either—although the clouds seemed so close that it made it difficult to be sure. The most telling sign of disuse was the dense network of thick, prickly vines that covered the walls.

"No one's lived here for years," said Emiline, pulling at her mousebelt. She reached the dark wooden door, unsheathed her knife, and started to cut away the creepers.

"I don't want to even think about what it's like inside," exclaimed Drewshank, surveying the building.

"It looks like it's been closed up for ages," added Scratcher. He tried to pull open the shutters to a window, but they were securely locked. "We'll have to break through the door."

Emiline pulled at the vines, which came away easily, and found that the door was sodden.

"It's almost rotten," she said excitedly, sliding her knife into the wood with ease. "Give me a hand!"

With a firm push from all three, the door twisted on its hinges and plunged in with a thump. A thick plume of dust lifted into the air, and a smell of damp foulness blew into their faces.

"What a choice," said Drewshank, "out here in the rain, or in there with the smell of a thousand rotten eggs!"

"At least it's dry," said Emiline, stepping into the dim hallway. Musty velvet drapes hung from the ceiling, and cobwebs swung down from every feature. Glass lamps were fixed to the walls, and after a brief inspection, Emiline realized they were still full of oil. She lit them without a second thought, and immediately the house felt more welcoming, bathed in a warm glow.

Emiline headed on up a narrow corridor to an open wooden door, which was creaking slightly with the wind now bustling through the house. Emiline crept forward and peered around it. She felt a shiver ripple down her back. The room smelled awful and was almost shrouded in darkness, the only light being thin shafts of grey that scythed their way through the shutters.

"Hello," she whispered, somewhat instinctively, before

squeezing her nose shut with her fingertips. There was no reply.

Emiline's eyes traced around the spot-lit areas: there was a bookshelf; a painting of pyramids; a candlestick holder with cobwebs running out from its metal lip to the wall; and there was the back of a squat armchair, a ruffled pillow sitting on its top. She stepped into the room and heard the floorboards squeal.

"What have you found?" shouted Scratcher from the hallway, realizing Emiline had gone in.

"Not much!" she replied nasally, bumping into a wooden table hidden by the dark. "Fancy helping me open these shutters?"

Scratcher appeared at her side.

"Oh, it stinks!" he exclaimed, before gazing around the small room. The two paced carefully to the windows, where they found thick iron bolts securing the shutters. With a sharp tug, the rusting metal bars loosened their grip and slid across. Scratcher teased his fingers into the cracks of the wood and pulled the shutters open.

A burst of grey light flooded the room. Dust flitted

here and there, muddying the air like dirt clouds in a pond. Emiline turned and saw the full extent of the room. It was dark red in color, though the years of neglect had taken their toll, and paint was peeling from the walls. A simple lamp hung from the ceiling — a half-burnt candle still visible through its glass panels — and bookshelves littered the walls, filled with hardy leather-backed books.

Scratcher drew breath sharply, and Emiline's eyes darted to him.

"What," she said, watching him step backward awkwardly.

"The chair…," he stuttered, "the chair…"

He pointed fearfully to the armchair, and Emiline stepped around the table to get a better look. Her skin started to crawl. All she saw was a blackened, decomposed hand resting on the chair's arm, but that was enough. She slammed her hand over her mouth and turned away, her stomach heaving.

"Captain!" shouted Scratcher, shielding his eyes. "I think we've found what we came here for!"

The captain wandered into the room nonchalantly and realized something was up with the mousekeepers.

"You all right?" he asked.

Both Emiline and Scratcher pointed to the armchair while staring resolutely in the opposite direction. Drewshank shuffled around the table and finally saw the rotten body in all its glory. He made a loud gulp, and his eyes started to water. It was safe to say that he wished he'd been more prepared.

The body was sitting upright in the way old people do when they accidentally doze off to sleep, but it barely resembled a human anymore. The skin was sunken, shriveled, and leathery, and bones protruded around the ribs—poking through the thin moth-eaten clothes that still remained on the corpse.

"She's dead then," said Drewshank, screwing up his face.

"I'd say so," replied Emiline, desperately trying to restrain the morbid fascination that made her want to sneak another look.

"What's Mousebeard going to think about that?" said Scratcher.

"Hmm, well, I think we should make pains to look

around more carefully," added Drewshank, walking away from the chair as fast as he could. "I'll check upstairs…"

Emiline started to follow him but instead turned to a bookshelf.

"She was a mouser," said Emiline with some surprise. "Look, there's the *Guide to Mousebones*, the *Mouse Fossil Record*, and even the *Mouse Trapper's Handbook*. I reckon there's a lot about this old lady that we don't know."

"So she liked mice!" said Scratcher. "Big deal; most people do."

"I know, but somehow she cursed Lovelock and Mousebeard. There must be clues about it here somewhere…."

"She just looks like a dead old lady to me," said Scratcher, fed up with the smell. "Even if she was a witch, so what? She's dead. Can we go now?"

Emiline pulled out another book, this one about rare mouse breeds, and something caught her attention. It was a sound that she'd heard many times before: the sound of mouseclaws on wood.

"There's a mouse in here!" she said excitedly.

"Where?" asked Scratcher.

"Listen…"

The two mousekeepers' eyes darted around the room, avoiding the dead body that lay so close. The noise was only faint, and slow moving, but it was definitely there. Emiline started pulling books off all the shelves, hoping to find any sign of life.

"It's got to be here…"

"Emiline!" whispered Scratcher, now kneeling on the floor. "It's staring at me!"

Emiline stopped in her tracks and stepped over to her friend. He was half under the table, and at the other side of the room, near the skirting board, a small mouse was shivering by a mousehole. It was no ordinary mouse: its body was aged and wrinkled, with barely any fur. Occasional wiry hairs towered out of its back and ears, and its twisted ancient nose twittered in the air as though tasting the smell of the new arrivals.

"Its eyes…," marveled Scratcher; "they're almost pure white!"

Emiline lowered herself to get a look at the creature. She tapped Scratcher's back in feverish excitement.

"It's the Methuselah Mouse!" she whispered. "This

must be the one they came here for all those years ago...they can live forever!"

The mouse continued to sniff the air. Its ears, which were initially alert, started to drop — a sure sign it was becoming less wary.

"You have any Ground Worm Bait?" asked Scratcher hopefully. "That might work...."

Emiline unhooked a small pouch on her mousebelt and handed it to him.

"Do you still not know anything?" she said, rolling her eyes. "You use that for feral mice — this mouse hasn't been in the wild for years. Much better to use Dried Gumbo Berries — the ones soaked in barley juice, of course."

Scratcher sighed, and he reluctantly took the mousebait. Emiline had a terrible habit of knowing almost everything about mice.

As he placed a small amount on the floor, not more than a meter from his hand, the Methuselah Mouse started to move. It made cautious steps — its rickety and weak legs clearly not as capable as they once were — but it was soon under the table and just a short distance from Scratcher.

"Now don't make a move yet," whispered Emiline. "Let it eat a little first...."

Scratcher twisted his head around sharply to stare angrily at Emiline.

"I know!" he snapped quietly.

The mouse started chewing at the berries. One of them filled its tiny paws, and its movements were so slow that it took ages for it to lift the berry to its mouth, but it was clearly hungry, and growing ever more confident.

Scratcher cautiously removed a mousebox from his belt and laid it on the ground, taking great pains not to make any quick movements. He then held out his hand, slowly moving it closer to the mouse.

"Steady...," whispered Emiline, wishing desperately it was herself making the catch.

As Scratcher's hand got within grasping range, the creature, most unexpectedly, started walking toward it. With much care and fragility, the Methuselah Mouse then stepped up his fingers and gradually crawled its way onto his palm, where it stopped and settled.

"It likes me," he said, dumbfounded. Mice usually never showed him such respect.

"I imagine it's been lonely," said Emiline, looking closely at the strange old mouse. Scratcher stroked it gently and found its skin to be incredibly dry and leathery.

"Not the prettiest of creatures," he added, "but I like it all the same!"

Scratcher attempted to place it in the comfort of his mousebox, but the mouse became agitated, working its way backward up Scratcher's arm.

"He doesn't want to go in," said Emiline.

Scratcher's smile turned to dismay.

"But I can't carry him!" he replied.

"Why not? I manage with Portly."

"But it's all old and wrinkly...."

"Scratcher!" laughed Emiline. "What's that got to do with it?"

"Oh...nothing," he said unhappily, knowing he was being unreasonable. He opened a pocket inside his raincoat and showed it to the mouse. It lifted its nose slightly, twitched it a few times, and slowly clawed its way in.

"Perfect," he said huffily.

⇒ ✳ ⇐

Mousebeard stretched his arm out fully and caught the exhausted Onloko Mouse, just as it looked set to career into the choppy sea. Its tired wings flopped over his fingers, and with a short sigh it closed its eyes and fell straight to sleep. A soaked message was secured around its body by a thin leather strap, and Mousebeard started to untie the bindings with his thick, calloused fingers.

"Algernon?" called the pirate. "You know about this?"

Algernon was busy tinkering with one of his inventions in Mousebeard's cabin, and at the sound of the pirate's voice lifted up his head.

"What?" he replied, removing his magnifying goggles as he walked out on deck. His eyes lit up when he saw the mouse.

"A Red-winged Onloko? A leather message harness...," stuttered Algernon; "that's our man Horatio Spires for sure."

"He's come to no harm then," said Mousebeard.

The pirate unscrolled the letter, written in neat and controlled handwriting. The ink had started to run down the page, so he shielded it with his hand before reading it aloud.

*Dearest Jonathan,*

*I apologize profusely for failing to make our rendezvous, but I had to secure one final piece of information before leaving Grandview. I deemed it far more important than the matter of my escaping, and you will understand that soon enough. I dare not write my findings here for fear of my mouse being intercepted — I know I am being searched for, and it is only a matter of time before they finally place me. I sought sanctuary in Hamlyn, but it was a mistake — there are soldiers everywhere, and the Old Town Guard has taken control of the port.*

*I fear I may not live to tell you in person what I know, so I have placed my findings in a tin box in Algernon's usual drop-off point. He'll understand exactly where I mean.*

*Do not hesitate in returning to Hamlyn using whatever force or means necessary, my friend. I have no care for my own safety, but you must receive this information before it is too late.*

*Your faithful friend,*
*Horatio*

Mousebeard stepped back and passed the note to Algernon.

"Is it from his hand?"

"It certainly looks like it," replied Algernon, fretting. "We must make for Hamlyn as soon as we can. Oh I don't know why he thought it was a good idea to go there...."

⇒ ✳ ⇐

As soon as Emiline returned to the *Silver Shark*, she knew something was up. Sailors were readying the vessel for voyage, and the working mice had been released. Algernon stood waiting for them, oblivious to the rain that had soaked him through.

"What's wrong?" asked Emiline.

"Bad news from Spires...," said Algernon.

"Bad news?" said Scratcher, concerned.

"He's trapped in Hamlyn."

"Hamlyn?" exclaimed Drewshank. "What's the old fool gone there for?"

"I imagine it was his only choice," said Emiline. "What are we going to do about it?"

At the sight of the new arrivals, Mousebeard rushed on deck from his cabin. His face looked desperate for news.

"What did you find?" he asked.

"The woman was dead," said Drewshank.

Mousebeard's excitement immediately dwindled.

"But we did find this," said Scratcher shakily, taking a few steps forward. He still hadn't gotten used to the pirate, and his nerves were affecting his speech. He pushed his hand within his jacket and withdrew the Methuselah Mouse, shielding it from the rain with his fingers. Its subdued eyes peered around, and its ears perked up. Mousebeard was speechless. He held out his hands, allowing Scratcher to place the mouse within his massive palms.

The Methuselah Mouse started to shiver, and its rough skin wrinkled up. Its nose twitched and sniffed at Mousebeard, who lifted it to get a closer look.

"After all these years," said Algernon, walking closer, "that was what you came here for, and now you have it."

"In my very hands," Mousebeard said quietly, as though all his years as a pirate had fallen away from him.

The Methuselah Mouse moved up the pirate's arm and began clawing at the dense beard in front of it. Gradually, it pushed its way into the matted hair and disappeared from view.

"Thank you, Scratcher," said Mousebeard awkwardly. He seemed utterly confused by the mouse's appearance and actions.

"At least it's safe in your beard," said Scratcher. "Better there than in my jacket pocket!"

"It is," replied Mousebeard. "Algernon, have you discussed our plans?"

Algernon shook his head.

"We have to rescue Horatio," said Mousebeard. "He's found something important and we have no time to lose. We sail straightaway!"

Drewshank suddenly spoke out.

"This is ludicrous," he said. "To Hamlyn? We'd never get away with it! I'm all up for clearing our names, but that's too much of a risk!"

"It's a risk we have to take," said Algernon.

"No it's not," said Drewshank firmly.

Algernon was slightly taken aback by Drewshank's authority.

"What else do you propose?" he said.

"I know Hamlyn well. I have a better proposition. Take us in the submarine, and drop us at the docks right under their noses. Emiline and Scratcher will come with me, I'm sure."

He looked at the mousekeepers with a smile. Mousebeard watched their reactions.

"A chance to visit Hamlyn again?" said Emiline. "I wouldn't miss it!"

"It will be dangerous," said Algernon.

"Surely less dangerous than taking a great big silver ship?" said Drewshank.

"Subterfuge rather than force," said Mousebeard, thinking aloud. "Maybe he's right, Algernon?"

"I'm in," said Scratcher, his confidence rising.

Algernon stood silently for a few seconds, then agreed wholeheartedly.

"It's a plan, then," said Drewshank. "But where shall we meet afterward?"

"After Stormcloud, I'd intended to sail to the Mural Isles. There's someone I need to speak to there...."

"That sounds as good a place as any to meet up," said Algernon.

"Perfect," said Drewshank. "Fenwick, you stay here and help our friend Mousebeard. Make sure he gets there safely."

Fenwick attempted a smile. He would have much rather traveled with Drewshank.

Mousebeard shook Drewshank's hand vigorously.

"Bring back Horatio in one piece," he said, his grip threatening to crush Drewshank's fingers.

"We'll do everything we can," exclaimed Emiline.

Mousebeard threw his arms in the air and shouted out to his sailors.

"Ready yourselves, men, we have a new direction! Take us south! There's no time to waste!"

# The Stripy Sand Mouse

AN INQUISITIVE, SHORT-HAIRED BROWN MOUSE THAT, DESPITE LIVING IN THE desert, gets frustrated when sand gets caught in its fur. It's nocturnal by nature, spending much of its time in burrows underground while the sun is at its hottest.

This mouse is very easy to pick out from others because of the prominent lighter stripes of fur on its back. These stripes act as excellent camouflage amongst the dunes, but its beautiful fur has been greatly sought after amongst collectors throughout the ages. Numbers remaining in the wild are sadly very small because of this.

MOUSING NOTES:

*Due to being on the brink of extinction, this mouse is not allowed in any collection!*

# A Different Hamlyn

E MILINE SLID OUT OF THE SUBMARINE, THE DIM GLOW emanating from Hamlyn providing some assistance. The tall island rose up before her, with the lights of its streets and buildings flickering like a constellation in the night sky.

"It's so quiet…," she muttered, reaching out and placing her hand on the quayside. She looked around, noting the sentry points and watchtowers at the harbor entrance. There was no sign of anyone.

"All's clear!" she said, lowering her mouth to the submarine's hatch.

With a short hop, she launched herself onto the cobblestones and ran for cover against a low wall that divided the quayside from the street. She'd only been to Hamlyn once before, but even in that brief visit it was noticeable how rowdy the place had been. Everything seemed different now. There was barely any drunken cheering coming from the many inns, and even less singing ringing out to muffle the cawing of the seagulls.

Scratcher's head appeared from the submarine, and Emiline signaled for him to make a move. He jumped to the quayside and darted across to where his friend was waiting.

"What's happened to the place?" said Scratcher, surveying the street, where at this time of night you'd normally find pirates and drunkards falling over and waging war among themselves.

"It's far too quiet," replied Emiline. "Where is everyone?"

With a soft clunk, the hatch of the submarine closed tight, and Drewshank leapt across and caught up with the mousekeepers.

"Oh this isn't right!" he exclaimed, placing his hand on Scratcher's shoulder. In the background, the sound of bubbles breaking the water's surface let them know Algernon had returned to the seabed. "Spires mentioned the

Old Town Guard had taken over, but I never imagined it would be like this!"

Drewshank lifted his head over the wall to look up the street and immediately dropped it back again.

"And here they come!" he whispered, waving his hand downward through the air to let Scratcher and Emiline know they should crouch lower.

The noise of marching boots grew louder and louder, until it sounded as though the guards were right behind them. Emiline felt her heart rate quicken, and Scratcher pushed his back firmly against the wall.

"Get out there and stay out there!" ordered one of the Old Town Guard, before he stamped down violently.

"But General Mordiford, it's my day off!" pleaded a young boy.

Drewshank recognized the boy's voice, and his expression turned to one of concern.

"I'll have none of this insolence!" barked the man. "Your position is to keep us informed of the weather, and you'll do that until your last living breath! Do I make myself clear?"

"Yes, sir," replied the boy sheepishly.

"And if I see you leave your post again, I'll have you stripped of your status and posted back to Old Town, do you hear?"

"Yes, sir..."

With a shouted order, the Old Town Guard marched onward. Emiline looked to Drewshank as she heard the boy shuffle alongside the wall just a few meters away. Drewshank shook his head at her to calm her. The boy let out a slight grumble and clambered onto the wall before jumping down. Scratcher slid sideways instinctively and took hold of the knife at his side. The boy was wearing a strange helmet and in his right hand was a long stick with a fish attached to its end.

Drewshank leaned forward.

"Mildred!" he whispered. "Psssst! Mildred!"

The boy glanced to his left and rubbed his eyes. He then stepped back so his legs were pressed to the wall, and looked left and right as he sidled closer without lifting his feet from the ground.

"Mr. Drewshank!" he said excitedly, while staring straight ahead and trying not to look suspicious. "What in the name of Guidolfo Jones are you doing here?"

"We're looking for someone...," the captain replied quietly.

"Just like all those folk are out looking for you!" said Mildred from the corner of his mouth. "You're in real trouble! In all the papers..."

"Don't I know it, but what's happened to this place?"

"The Guard have ruined it," whispered Mildred, swinging his dried fish as though checking the air conditions. "The Mayor of Old Town has taken over. We don't get half the ships we used to! I hate it."

"Well, you might be able to help us, Mildred," said Drewshank hopefully.

For the first time, Mildred's will broke, and he darted a look at Drewshank.

"I might?"

"Have you seen anyone who looks like a butler land here lately?"

"Butlers, Mr. Drewshank? We don't see many of them around here."

"So you haven't—"

The boy interrupted. "But there was someone who had little glasses and shiny shoes.... I thought he looked a bit odd getting off a boat with shiny shoes on....Butlers have shiny shoes, don't they? The rest of him was covered by a big grey cloak though, so I couldn't be sure."

"That's him!" whispered Emiline. "It's got to be!"

"Any idea where we might find this man?" Drewshank asked.

"I think so, Mr. Drewshank. My sister works at the Antelope Inn at the top of Pleasant Street, and she told me they'd gotten a new guest with shiny shoes. She hadn't seen such shiny shoes, she said. I bet that's your man. You know, there haven't been many visitors to Hamlyn in the past few months, so when a new guest arrives we get quite excited. Times aren't easy here, Mr. Drewshank!"

"No, I can see that," he said sadly.

"So what's our plan?" asked Scratcher.

"To be on the safe side, we should first find the box Spires left for us," said Drewshank.

"But we can't waste time like that," pleaded Emiline. "What if something happens to him?"

"We could split up, Captain," suggested Scratcher. "I'll get the box, you two go and find Mr. Spires..."

Drewshank looked at the boy.

"That's what we'll do. You remember what Algernon told you?"

Scratcher nodded.

"And I know how to find Pleasant Street," said Drewshank, "so if you're happy with that, Emiline?"

"Of course...," she said.

"Then that's settled," said Drewshank.

"It ain't safe out there now," whispered Mildred worriedly. "The Guard will be on the lookout for any movement after dark. There's a curfew for another few hours yet...."

"We can't worry about that," said Drewshank, "but thank you, Mildred. You don't know how useful you've been!"

"Anything to help you, Mr. Drewshank! I won't tell a soul about you all, honest!" he added, puffing out his chest and straightening his helmet.

"Is the street clear?" asked Emiline hurriedly.

Mildred scanned the docks before nodding.

"No soldiers in sight," he said.

"You ready?" she asked Scratcher and Drewshank.

"Ready as ever...," said Scratcher.

They stood up as one, and Emiline gave her friend a light kiss on the cheek.

"Don't get yourself caught this time," she said, before rolling over the wall.

"I won't," he replied, blushing.

"Thanks, Mildred," they all said, as they parted company and ran off up the dark streets.

Mildred looked at the dead fish on the end of his stick. Its tail was curling to the left.

"Well I never," he muttered quietly. "Looks like we'll have rain in the morning."

⇒ ✳ ⇐

The short journey to Pleasant Street proved easier than they could have hoped for. The narrow streets of Hamlyn provided ample cover, and not once did Drewshank or Emiline meet any trouble. Pleasant Street had once been the richest street on the island, with many buildings built of white stone — a rarity on Hamlyn. It was a place for those who sought enjoyment, with inns and shops aplenty, but in the current climate it was suffering. Shops were boarded up, or had signs on their fronts saying "Only open on Wednesday," and the inns were doing a dismal trade.

The Antelope Inn rested at the far end of the street, with its overhanging second floor jutting out farther than the rest of the buildings. Its sign, showing a proud antelope figurehead at the front of a ship, was swinging gently in the breeze, and Emiline was the first to see it.

"How are we going to let Mr. Spires know we're here?" she asked, as Drewshank stepped into a dark alley to catch his breath. She waited for his reply, forever casting her eyes up and down the road.

"If he's still here, that is…," he replied. "That letter would have been sent well over a week ago. And unfortunately for us, the owners will be wary of anyone out and about at this time of night."

"So we wait here?" asked Emiline.

"I guess so. The sky is already heading to dawn, so there should only be an hour or so before we start to see people out and about. We'll move then — you might as well make yourself comfortable for a bit."

Emiline stepped into the alley and slid down next to

Drewshank, making herself as comfortable as possible on the gravel surface. There was straw, and dirt, and all manner of unmentionable substances littering the floor, but she tried not to think about it. Instead, she let Portly out from her mousebox and allowed him some exercise. His whiskers twitched as he raced up her shoulders and under her hair.

> ✳ ⋖

Scratcher reached the graveyard in good time, and he immediately wished he hadn't gone by himself. The ominous iron gates shrieked as he forced them open into the overgrown scrub beyond. A muddy path led away into the darkness, with a jumble of gravestones popping up like rotten teeth at its edges. Despite the sky becoming lighter, it just made him more scared and more aware of what he couldn't quite see.

He walked slowly on, listening to the crunch of the floor beneath his feet. His eyes were often taken by dark shapes zipping along the ground, but he realized—or hoped—that they were just mice and nothing more sinister.

There were hundreds of gravestones, and the tired and rain-worn names of the dead took far too long to read for Scratcher's liking. Following Algernon's directions, he stepped off the path at the grave of Sara Gutheim and rushed along the scrubby grass. Eerie tombs covered with angels of the dead loomed high, and as soon as he found himself at the farthest reaches of the graveyard, he caught a glimpse of a broken wall, just as had been described.

He carried on walking for a few minutes, feeling the damp seeping into his shoes, before he found what he was after. Part hidden by the descending branches of an overgrown tree, the grave of Onquin Dandiprat was different from most because of the mass of wild roses rambling over its mound.

Scratcher wasted no time; he pulled the roses away, scaring a small Bearded Mouse in the process, and found the dull metal casket. It was joined to the gravestone by a metal chain, and he pulled it out to get a closer look. His eyes fell on the lock, broken and cracked and, upon raising the lid, he felt his stomach start to freefall. There was no letter inside, just the feeling that someone had gotten to it first. Someone knew of Spires's whereabouts, and knew of what he wanted to tell Mousebeard. Scratcher threw the casket down in disgust and felt his blood boil. He had to run to his friends, and get there fast.

⇒ ✳ ⇐

As the sun lifted higher into the sky, the sound of day-to-day ritual once again filled the streets of Hamlyn. Emiline and Drewshank eventually stepped out onto Pleasant Street, taking every effort to look as natural amongst the townsfolk as possible. They walked toward the Antelope Inn and noticed the door was open wide for custom. The smell of fried food drifted out onto the street, and Emiline's stomach started to rumble.

"Here we are then," said Drewshank.

Emiline had already walked inside. It was grander than Algernon's inn had been, with the main door leading into a highly decorated parlor and a grandfather clock set against the farthest wall. At its edge was a twisting wooden staircase, which rose in a gentle curve to the two floors above. The inn was notable for its almost deathly silence — the only noises coming from the kitchen, where an occasional clatter of pans rang out.

"Upstairs?" quizzed Emiline, looking at some of the paintings that hung from the walls.

"I guess so, and if they only have a few guests, as Mildred said, I'm sure it will be easy to find him if he's here," replied Drewshank.

Suddenly a door slammed shut on the ground floor, and Emiline and Drewshank jumped into hiding under the staircase. The only window on the ground floor cast a wide shadow in their direction, so they were safely hidden. In just a few seconds, a young girl walked past carrying a tray of food and a jug of water. She rushed to the stairs and started climbing at quite a rate.

"Mildred's sister!" whispered Emiline. "Carrying food for a guest?"

"Let's follow her," said Drewshank, leaving cover, "but let's be quiet, eh?"

They darted out and up onto the stairwell, taking unusually dainty steps so as not to make a sound. As they reached the first floor, a loud scream came from above, followed by the sound of a plate smashing. Emiline turned to Drewshank, and both immediately suspected the worst. Forgetting any attempts at being quiet, they charged up the stairs.

As they reached the second floor, the girl came hurtling out of a room, tears flooding from her eyes. She barely saw Drewshank and Emiline as she flew by. Emiline reached the door from where she'd come and pushed it wide. For a split second she froze in fear.

"Mr. Spires!" she cried, rushing into the room.

The butler lay on the floor, propped up awkwardly against the bed. His hand clutched his chest, and a red stain was spreading across his shirt. His head was tilted back, his glasses cracked and sitting askew on his nose. Emiline placed her hand on his cheek and noticed his chest was barely rising as he struggled to breathe.

When Drewshank walked in, he understood all too well what had happened.

"Is he still alive, Emiline?" he asked firmly.

"Barely. I think," she said, her words faltering as she struggled to come to terms with the situation.

"Why are...you...here?" said Spires, his words breathless and strained. "My letter...I warned you...not to come here..."

"But you didn't...," said Emiline, confused.

"I...I..."

The butler's words stopped as his breathing weakened.

"We can't hang around; we have to leave immediately," ordered Drewshank.

"Captain?" pleaded Emiline, as the butler gasped for air. She watched his hand rise and start to push against her.

"What is it?" she asked softly, trying desperately not to notice the bloodstain growing on his once-crisp white shirt.

The butler failed to speak. His eyes seemed distant and clouded, but he continued to push his hand at her.

Drewshank walked farther into the room and realized that all the butler's possessions were gone. There was nothing but his bed linen and the signs of a struggle. He tugged at Emiline's shoulder.

"We have to leave, Emiline," he said forcefully. "Can you stand, Spires?"

The butler swallowed painfully and shook his head.

"Emiline, we have to go!" Drewshank said again. "There's nothing we can do now. We have to leave him…"

As he said this, he heard people on the stairs, and he jumped to the door.

"Soldiers!" he snarled. "Emiline!"

"I can't leave him like this," she said tearfully, placing her hand at the back of Spires's head. Once again the butler pushed his hand against Emiline, but finally he managed to get her to realize what it was he wanted. In his fingers was a bloodstained handkerchief. He forced it into her hand and gave a weak smile. His chest shuddered, and his eyes closed.

"Mr. Spires!" she cried, gripping his shoulder.

Drewshank slammed the door shut and pulled across a table to block anyone's entry. He smashed his fist against its panels.

"Captain," said Emiline, tears welling in her eyes. "I think he's gone."

Spires's hand dropped slowly away from his chest, and Emiline saw the horrible stab wound for the first time. She crumpled down onto the floor, letting tears flow freely down her cheeks. Drewshank walked over and knelt down with his arm around her. He looked at the butler and wondered what awaited them.

"I'm sorry, Emiline," he said warmly. "I know he was your friend. He was a good man."

The door started to splinter as the soldiers smashed into it with the butts of their rifles. The noise was deafening.

"But he didn't deserve this," said Emiline, wiping the tears from her eyes, oblivious to the threat at the door. "They didn't need to do this...."

Drewshank sighed. He watched the door break open. The table lurched forward, wood shards flew across the room, and suddenly he was staring straight into the eyes of three soldiers, their guns trained on him.

⇒ ✳ ⇐

Scratcher ran as hard as he could. Hamlyn was busier now that the nightly curfew had ended, although it was still nowhere near as crowded as he remembered. He asked a fishmonger for directions to Pleasant Street, and after a brief discussion about how it wasn't the same since the Guard had taken over, he made his way there without pausing for breath.

His worst fears were realized when he found the street blocked off. Lines of soldiers stood guard at either end, and a small crowd of sellers and shop owners bustled angrily in between, remonstrating at the authorities for making life even harder for them.

Scratcher walked calmly up to one of the soldiers.

"Excuse me, sir," he asked, clutching his hands behind his back. "Why is the street blocked?"

"We've caught some of those fugitives from Old Town," replied the soldier gruffly. "You'd do well to watch what happens to their kind and not get involved in stuff like that yourself!"

"Oh," said Scratcher, caring little for the lecture. "What were they doing here?"

The soldier shuffled his feet to get comfortable.

"Who knows?" he said. "They shouldn't have come here, though....I could have told them that for nothing. Biggest concentration of soldiers outside Old Town!"

Scratcher looked past the troops but saw nothing of his friends on the street. He was alone, with no idea of what to do next.

"What will happen to them?" he finally asked.

"Well, they escaped the gallows once, but they won't manage a second time," replied the soldier proudly. "I can assure you of that!"

Scratcher's memory flashed back to when he stood upon the scaffold, rope around his neck. He knew all too well what that felt like. He said his thanks to the soldier and walked away slowly. All he could think about was what he would say to Algernon.

⇒ ✳ ⇐

"Put your hands in the air, and stand slowly!" shouted the soldier.

Drewshank rose gradually, and Emiline followed. Despite the situation, Emiline didn't feel scared. Tears were still clinging to her cheeks, and she only felt sad; not just for the butler, but for anyone who would do such a thing to him.

Footsteps could be heard coming from the stairs, and the soldiers separated to let someone through.

"Of course," said Drewshank, watching a person he knew very well walk in. "Lady Pettifogger..."

Beatrice Pettifogger entered the room, a wide smile on her face. Her eyes were sparkling, as always, and Drewshank snorted in disgust.

"You did this?" he spat.

Pettifogger paced around the room, touched Emiline's damp cheek, and observed the butler's body.

"Not me personally, Devlin," she said, laughing. "You know I'd have nothing to do with such a base act. But this man has been responsible for countless deaths—maybe as many as that infernal Mousebeard himself. He deserved no better...."

"No better?" cried Emiline.

"But I'm surprised you came here so readily," said Pettifogger. "Or maybe you actually thought that the butler's message was from his own hand? Have we fooled you once again, Captain?"

Drewshank squeezed his eyes shut and exhaled angrily.

"What have you become?" he asked. He always knew she was trouble, but even this, he thought, was beyond her.

Pettifogger walked around to Drewshank and smiled up at him.

"I've become what I always wanted," she said, tilting her head down. "I am powerful!"

Drewshank threw his hand down to his waist to draw

his sword, but the soldiers leapt forth immediately and hit him on the head with their rifle butts.

"That was stupid, Devlin," she said, as she watched his hands being bound. "I could have made things better for you. But not now…"

She gave him one final look before leaving the room.

"Tie up the girl too," she ordered from the landing. "Bring them to the Trading Center and lock them in the cells. I want to question them myself before we send them to Old Town."

# The Jouster Mouse

NOT TO BE CONFUSED WITH THE MINIATURE UNICORN MOUSE, THE MALE *Jouster mouse is endowed with an enormous horn protruding from the top of its head. It's a particularly strong horn too, and it is used in fights to the death with other males when searching for a mate. Not to be outdone, the female has an equally impressive horn, but it will never use its horn aggressively, as it is much more civilized and grown-up. Despite their less aggressive nature, the females do watch the males fight, and will often crowd around anxiously to get a good view.*

### MOUSING NOTES:

*The Jouster Mouse makes a fine addition to any collection, as its specialist needs are relatively few — the main requirement being adequate space to contain its horn. Beware, though: never, under any circumstances, should you keep two males together. It has been known to end in a horrific mess!*

# The Mouse Trading Center

T HROW THEM IN," GRUMBLED THE SNEERING PRISON
guard. Emiline tumbled down the few steps into
the prison cell, with Drewshank pushed in shortly after,
and the door slammed behind. There was no light, and
the prisoners sat down, finding it easier than struggling
blindly in the dark. The floor was cold to touch, and
Emiline pulled her jacket under her so as not to freeze.

"I'd really like to go a year without being thrown into
prison," muttered Drewshank grimly, waiting desperately
for his eyes to get used to the conditions.

"I can't believe Mr. Spires is dead," said Emiline, feeling
his handkerchief in her pocket.

"They won't get away with it," he replied. "I just can't believe we were so easily fooled."

"Mousebeard won't let them, I know it," she said, holding back the tears once more.

"Mousebeard?"

"Of course Mousebeard," said Emiline.

"Who said that?" asked Drewshank, puzzled.

"What?" replied Emiline.

"Mousebeard...," said Drewshank again, looking around fruitlessly, as he couldn't see a thing. "I didn't say that!"

"You did," said Emiline, confused.

"I never...who's there?" asked Drewshank.

Emiline fell silent.

"Who's there?" he asked again.

Emiline found herself staring vainly into the darkness. The voice spoke again. It was sure, if a touch weary, and tinged with a slight and unusual accent that Emiline hadn't noticed before.

"So you know Mousebeard?" it said.

"What if we do?" said Emiline nervously. "Who are you?"

The stranger paused before continuing.

"A prisoner, like yourselves."

"Why not introduce yourself before scaring the blazes out of people," snapped Drewshank angrily. "It's not like we could see you in here. You okay, Emiline?"

"Yes," she replied.

They heard the prisoner move, his shoes scuffing on the floor. Emiline clenched her fists, and Drewshank slid onto his knees in readiness.

"I'm not your enemy," the voice said.

"Prove it," said Emiline. "Why are you here?"

"Most likely the same reason you are...."

"Stop playing games," ordered Drewshank, whose patience was wearing thin.

"My name's Indigo," he said assuredly. "And you are?"

"Devlin Drewshank..."

"Ahh, now it makes sense," said Indigo; "you're one of Old Town's most wanted. I've read about your escape—quite a feat."

Drewshank started to warm to their fellow prisoner.

"And the girl's...sorry...your name?" asked Indigo.

"Emiline," she said. "I'm a mousekeeper. And once again, why are you in here?"

"Hmm," he replied teasingly. "I was paying a little too

much attention to the darker side of this Mouse Trading Center. I couldn't think of a more inappropriate name for the place."

"I don't follow you," said Emiline.

"I came here not so long ago," admitted Drewshank sagely. "I knew then that there was more here than a simple shop."

"Much more...," said Indigo.

With a short scraping noise, a spark burst into life, and Indigo's form was lit up in the corner. Emiline and Drewshank blinked as their eyes adjusted. Indigo sat with his knees up, a small lamp in one hand, and he gazed straight at them. He had bright green eyes, and his long black hair fell down across his face to where it was tied loosely at the back. Emiline realized he was only a few years older than her, but he seemed a lot more when he talked.

"This place will be the downfall of all the mousing world," he said darkly.

"What?" said Emiline.

"They're here, aren't they?" asked Drewshank.

"The Golden Mice?" said Indigo. "Of course they are..."

"You know about them?" asked Emiline.

Indigo laughed. "I do," he said. "Do you know about the breeding program?"

"Huh?" said Drewshank.

"They've been crossbreeding the Golden Mice to try and gain a greater yield of gold."

"Crossbreeding?" questioned Emiline. "Surely not…"

Indigo smiled.

"You really don't know half of what they're up to, do you?" he said.

"It would seem not," replied Drewshank. "Do tell…"

"There are factories being built right across the world, from Midena to the far-off lands past the Great Sea, and all with one purpose — to utilize the Golden Mouse's unique fur. This Trading Center was just the beginning, where they practiced and perfected the breeding. From what I can tell, they've already successfully bred count-less Golden Mice, and shipments have been sent out for harvesting. But this is where the crossbreeding comes in. Imagine a Golden Mouse the size of a Giant Tusk Mouse — what would that animal's fur be worth?"

"No!" said Emiline. "It would never work!"

"Is that what you think?" laughed Indigo. "Trust me, I've seen some of the mistakes...."

"Mistakes?" stuttered Drewshank.

"They still keep them here locked up, like grisly exhibition pieces of what not to do."

Indigo stopped talking, and he twisted a screw on his lamp to make it go out. The cell was plunged into darkness once more.

"I only have a small amount of oil," he said.

"I'm surprised they let you keep that," said Drewshank. "They took everything of ours, including Emiline's mouse."

"They didn't check my boot," he said wisely.

"So when you say mistakes...," said Emiline.

"Chimeras, monsters, call them what you like."

"Monsters?"

Indigo made a sigh and tried not to sound annoyed.

"Yes, monsters. Sometimes you don't know what will happen as a result of the crossing of species. There are creatures in this place that would make your skin crawl."

"You seem to know so much about this place," said

Drewshank inquisitively. "Maybe you wouldn't mind explaining yourself?"

"I was one of the mousekeepers here...."

"I see," interrupted Drewshank.

"But I stuck my nose in too far. They don't like people knowing what goes on."

"So you know a way out?"

"There's just the one—through the front door. Which means you'd have to get through locked doors and armed soldiers. I'm sorry to say, there's very little chance of escape."

"In my experience, there's always a means of escape," said Drewshank boldly.

"I didn't say it was impossible, Drewshank. Do you have a means of getting off the island if you do get out?"

"We do," said Emiline confidently.

"I think it's time we struck a deal, then," said Indigo. "I get you out of here, you get me off the island."

"How do we know we can trust you?" asked Emiline.

"You don't, but that's a risk you need to take...."

"Mr. Mysterious," quipped Drewshank.

"Maybe," replied Indigo, "but trusting me is surely an easier option than living in this prison cell."

"I wouldn't disagree with you. What do you think, Emiline?"

She hesitated before agreeing.

"No funny business, promise?" she said sternly.

"No funny business," he replied.

"Then I think you have a deal," said Drewshank triumphantly.

⇒ ❋ ⇐

The cell door chimed as it swung open against the wall, and a roly-poly guard stood silhouetted in the light of the passageway.

"Come on, Drewshank!" he growled, tapping a truncheon repeatedly against his leg. "Lady Pettifogger wants a word…."

"Oh, she does, does she?" muttered Drewshank, blinking wildly as his eyes came to terms with the situation. After a long time in the dark it felt as though he'd forgotten the very idea of light. He stood up slowly and trudged up the few steps to the door.

"Don't like the light, eh?" said the guard, poking Drewshank's back to force him out. He grabbed the door, pulled it shut, and twisted a giant key in its lock.

"I don't mind it, actually. I'd rather be in the dark than have to look at your ugly face," he replied. The truncheon hit into his back.

"Keep that fancy mouth of yours shut, or you'll get more of that," snapped the guard.

"Ah, do your worst," he muttered.

The guard pushed him onward, and Drewshank found himself negotiating a narrow corridor. The walls were painted white, and every few meters along, an iron door stood on each side; they all had small glass windows, though only a few showed any light from the inside.

"Keep your eyes out of them," barked the guard, watching Drewshank trying to catch sight of what lay beyond the doors. "You ain't here on a sightseeing trip! Turn left!"

Drewshank followed the corridor as the guard asked, and he soon found himself at another door.

"Open it!" said the guard, prodding Drewshank in the back once more.

He twisted the polished door handle and made his way in.

"My dear Devlin!" proclaimed Lady Pettifogger, standing against a wall at the far side. The room was more brightly lit than the corridor, and it was quite empty, apart from a wide iron table and a cluster of chairs. Once again, the walls were whitewashed and sterile-looking, with oil lamps dotted all around.

"Do sit down," she said.

Drewshank pulled a chair out and slid down onto its hard seat.

"You're not ones for luxury in this place, are you," he said caustically.

"I don't think you'll see much luxury anymore," she replied. "You're to be returned to Dire Street Prison in the next day or so."

"Now you really are spoiling me!"

"Only the best for Captain Drewshank! Our hospitality knows no bounds for a man of your stature."

Drewshank huffed. He didn't care much for Pettifogger's company or her conversation.

"So what *do* you want of me?" he said bluntly. "And where's Lord Butterbum in all this?"

Pettifogger smiled.

"You have such a way with words, Devlin," she said. "Alexander is off exploring for Isiah — some new discovery or something — and, of course, the reason you're here is I want to know where Mousebeard is. Now that you're the best of friends, I'm certain you have the answer."

Drewshank let out a dry laugh. In the current circumstances he realized he'd much rather have the pirate's company.

"I don't know where he is."

"How about that Algernon Mountjack then? I presume he's the one who managed to sneak you here with his infernal submarine?"

"Oh, do me a favor...," he said, crossing his arms in rebuttal.

"Have it your way then," said Pettifogger, her voice no longer playful. "I suppose your fellow prisoner has informed you of what we've achieved here?"

"That Indigo? He's not the chattiest of folk," he lied.

"Oh come on, Drewshank. I'm certain you know of our success in breeding the Golden Mouse. Old Town will soon be the power of Midena once more, thanks to our limitless supply of gold."

"If that's what you think, then you're a greater fool than I thought you were."

"We're not fools, Devlin...."

Lady Pettifogger walked to the door and called to the guard. In a few seconds a man had appeared and passed her a cage.

"See for yourself," she said proudly.

Drewshank watched as she placed the large cage on the table. Through the bars at its front he saw a mouse. The first thing that struck him was its size, which was at least as long as his forearm, and then he saw its pure golden fur sparkling intensely. It was undoubtedly a Golden Mouse, but it looked so unnatural and overgrown.

Drewshank moved his hand closer to touch it, but it reared frantically onto its haunches and lunged at the bars, baring its long fangs in the process. It took him totally by surprise, and he jumped, before slowly pushing his chair backward away from the table.

"What have you done?" he said. "You've bred a monster...."

"Oh, I assure you, that's nothing compared to some of

the mishaps we've had. But we're almost there now. This variation is at least manageable," she said.

"Manageable? Are you mad?"

"How simple you are!" she tutted. "The fur on this creature is worth three thousand schillings at least."

Drewshank had to admit that this was an awful lot of money, and he raised his eyebrows in acknowledgment of the fact. But then he realized it was a ludicrous exercise.

"There is absolutely no way you can get away with this. Absolutely no way!"

"Devlin, we already have gotten away with it. The original Golden Mice that you helped steal are in safekeeping in Old Town, ready for the Illyrians to collect them when they choose. They won't suspect a thing."

"But Mousebeard will," he said assuredly.

"Will he indeed?" she replied knowingly. "If only you could tell him. It's a shame you'll be dead before you get the chance."

Drewshank started to scrape his fingers along his palms in anger.

"So back to the question I asked you at the start of this

wonderful conversation," she said, picking up the cage and moving to the door. "Where exactly is that pirate?"

"I have no idea," he said firmly.

"Well, it would appear that you really have signed your own death warrant this time."

Lady Pettifogger left the room and shouted for the guard.

"It was nice knowing you," she said, striding away.

≫ ❋ ≪

"Did you see what the time was?" Indigo asked, as Drewshank was thrown back into the cell.

"You could ask me how I am first," he replied, suddenly blind again in the dark.

"What happened?" asked Emiline, desperate for news.

"I have no idea of the time," said Drewshank, "but I did see the fruits of their labor, and it's not a pretty sight."

"Really?" said Emiline, intrigued.

"A massive Golden Mouse—that seems to have little in the way of manners yet very large fangs!"

"No!" breathed Emiline in disbelief.

"I told you so," said Indigo. "They're a disaster waiting to happen."

"And we don't have long until we're sent to Old Town," added Drewshank, "so any plans of escape should be put into action now, I feel."

"That's why I asked the time.... How many guards were there?" said Indigo.

"Just the one, and Pettifogger."

"Then it's evening — we should make our move."

"Now?" asked Emiline.

She heard Indigo cross the cell, and she realized he'd walked over to the door.

"They have fewer guards inside at night — and the scientists working on the mice will have gone home a few hours ago. Give me a minute..."

"What are you up to?" asked Drewshank.

"Ever heard of Mousing Explosive?"

"Of course," said Emiline.

"If you just add a few ingredients to the mix, you get a much better kick...."

"Really?" she said.

"Yeah—amazing what you can fit in the base of your boot!"

"Are you sure we should be blowing things up?" asked Drewshank warily.

"Unless you have any better ideas," said Indigo.

Drewshank remained silent. He had none.

"Okay, close your ears and get ready to run. When it blows, head out to the left. Got it?"

"What then?" asked Drewshank. "We have no weapons."

"I'll get them...."

Before Indigo could finish talking, a bright flash lit up the room, and a thunderous boom echoed around its stark interior.

"Run!" he shouted.

The door swung wide, its lock blown to pieces, and small fragments of metal sprayed around the room.

Emiline and Drewshank rushed out of the cell, both of them finding the light hard to deal with. They reached a door and found it firmly locked. Drewshank charged into it with his shoulder, but it wouldn't budge.

Indigo, however, ran to the right along the corridor.

He glimpsed each door as he passed, and eventually he stopped at one where the light was on. It was the guardroom. He pulled the door open and rushed inside, beating the guard to his own truncheon, which was hanging on a hook by the door.

"What!" shouted the guard furiously, as Indigo smashed it down on his head, knocking him out cold. The man crumpled to the ground, and Indigo looked around. He knew the workings of the Trading Center well, and soon he found a bunch of keys on a table. He heard Drewshank shout for him — he knew their door would be locked — but there was one more thing to do yet.

Leaving the guardroom, he darted to another door just a few meters farther down. He knew exactly what awaited inside. He went in, smashed open a cupboard with the truncheon, and found what he was looking for. Inside lay his mousebox and belt, as well as Emiline's and Drewshank's belongings. He picked them all up and tucked them under his arm. But he couldn't leave just yet. At the end of the room was another door, more secure and stronger than even the cell door.

When he heard the frantic scraping coming from the

other side, the sound of claws on metal, he knew there was only one thing to do. Indigo put everything down and lifted his boot. With a small flick of a hook on its side, the heel shot around to reveal small compartments stuffed with all manner of objects. He found his last small lump of enhanced Mousing Explosive, pushed it into the lock, and drew out a short fuse. With a tiny spark the fuse caught fire, and Indigo collected his things and ran.

"Where have you been?" shouted Drewshank angrily as Indigo reached them. For the first time they got a good look at him. His clothes were typical of a mousekeeper, with a tight grey jacket and thick cotton trousers, but his olive skin revealed he was not from Midena.

"Here...," said Indigo, passing them their things.

Emiline hooked her belt around her waist and heard Portly squeak angrily from within. Thankfully, he was still in one piece. Indigo slotted a key into the door just as the second explosion boomed out.

"What was that?" said Drewshank, tying his sword around his waist.

"Just a going-away present for them," Indigo replied, grinning. "We'd better hurry...."

The door opened easily, and they ran out into yet another corridor.

"This way!" he called, running off at full speed.

They veered around a tight corner and suddenly found themselves face-to-face with two soldiers, their swords at the ready. Indigo held out his hand so that Emiline and Drewshank would stop behind him.

"You don't know what you're taking on," growled Indigo to the soldiers.

They laughed at him and stepped closer.

"I mean it," he said, and lowered a hand to the large mousebox hanging at his waist. His fingers found the latch and loosened the lid.

"Get him!" the soldiers shouted.

Indigo stood firm and flipped back the lid of his mousebox. As if they had springs in their heels, two mice jumped out and launched themselves at the soldiers.

Emiline gasped in amazement. The mice were Sharp-claws, but a rare kind, with a white stripe running from the tips of their noses to their tails. Their huge razor-sharp claws flicked out and slashed down at the soldiers' swords, slicing them cleanly into scraps of metal.

Indigo whistled, and the Sharpclaws jumped back to form a barrier between him and the soldiers, their claws at the ready.

"I told you," Indigo said calmly. "Now let us pass!"

The soldiers meekly shrank back against the wall, the fear of a Sharpclaw too much even for them.

"Thank you," he said, picking up the mice and placing them back in his mousebox. He called for Drewshank and Emiline to follow him, and they climbed a set of stairs that opened out into the Trading Center. The lights were off, but as they crashed loudly into the room, the noisy squeaking of caged mice rang out like a dawn chorus.

"There'll be many more soldiers patrolling outside," said Indigo, "and I doubt we'll be able to get past them all unscathed."

"What are a few soldiers?" said Drewshank, drawing his sword. "With those mice, we could take on the world!"

# The Heracles Mouse

A TITAN AMONG MICE, THE HERACLES MOUSE IS AS STRONG AS AN OX AND *almost as big, but its numbers in the wild are now very few. Difficult to tame and very aggressive, this mouse has never been a favorite of collectors, although its strength is known to have been employed by the ancient Olnar civilization for pulling plows and carrying heavy loads.*

### MOUSING NOTES

*Now so rare, the Heracles Mouse is soon to be added to the endangered species list, making it illegal for any collector to own one.*

# The Professor

K EEP US RIGHT ON THAT COURSE!" SAID MOUSEBEARD, lifting a telescope to his eye.

The Mural Isles were a cluster of small granite islands that towered out of the sea like stalagmites. The community that inhabited them lived not only in the series of tunnels and caves within the islands' cores, but also in long arching bridges stretching from one island to the next, enabling people to travel among them without taking to the water. Visible from miles away, the narrow tips of the islands were host to huge windmills spinning serenely in the powerful easterly winds.

"As beautiful as I'd been led to believe," he muttered.

Fenwick approached the pirate to let him know all was well.

"The crew's getting used to the speed of the ship now," he said. "Working like a treat. And your Rigger Mice seem better skilled than most."

"That's a good sign, Mr. Fenwick. It's always hard taking on a new crew."

Fenwick took a greater look at the islands they were approaching. He'd heard of the Mural Isles before, but only for their outstanding colonies of Sea Mice, not for the towers of windmills.

"They're quite something…," he said.

Mousebeard agreed.

"People have lived here for nearly thirty years now. The inhabitants use the windmills for power, and they need nothing from elsewhere. They live off the sea, harvesting natural resources. They even harness the sun and the wind to remove the salt from the sea to create drinking water. I always marvel at the ingenuity of these people."

"So this person we're after…"

"Professor Lugwidge," said Mousebeard.

"How's he gonna help us?"

Mousebeard scrunched his beard between his fingers and felt the Methuselah Mouse within, sleeping peacefully.

"Professor Lugwidge was my tutor at the Old Rodents' Academy. I haven't seen him for many years, but I should like to ask him just what he knows about the woman on Storm-cloud Island. He told me about her originally, after all."

"It sounds like you might have a score to settle...."

"You could well be right," said Mousebeard. "But in this instance knowledge is of more use to me than violence. I'll ask him nicely first..."

The *Silver Shark* lowered its sails and started to drift effortlessly with the current toward the islands.

"Pull us in near the boats," shouted Mousebeard, directing the helmsman with his hand. "And don't expect a warm welcome...; people will have heard of us."

As they drew closer, the creaking, whooping noise of the windmills became much louder. The sails were imposing to look at from below, and they seemed particularly uncomfortable spiked upon the tapering rock towers.

A ship of its size rarely came to the close-knit community of the Murals, and one as notorious as the *Silver Shark* was unwelcome. It passed numerous fishing vessels chained to wharves and jetties, drawing disconcerted stares from sailors, and with every bridge spanning the islands that passed overhead, a thin shadow flew over the deck.

Mousebeard walked to the edge of the ship and stepped up onto a ledge to look over the side. A band of six men had gathered; all were dressed in fishermen's outfits and looked unlikely soldiers. But they held weapons in their hands, and their faces showed they wanted nothing to do with the pirate.

"You can't land here," proclaimed one of the men. The sight of Mousebeard had shaken him, and his voice rattled unconvincingly.

Mousebeard laughed and took his hat off in an unusual display of courtly behavior.

"I've not come to ransack your homes," he said, desperately holding back the urge to laugh out loud. "I'm after Lugwidge. I was told he lives here...."

The men maintained their guarded approach.

"What if he does?" replied the man. "You've got no reason to come here."

"I have every reason to come here," snarled Mousebeard,

forgetting his intention to be nice. "If you know what's good for you, you'll go and get him."

The man turned to his side and whispered to his friend, who lowered his musket and rushed off. Mousebeard watched him disappear through a door in the side of the rocky tower.

"All right," said the man. "We're peaceful here — but just because we don't fight, doesn't mean we can't...."

Mousebeard's smile returned to his beard.

"I know those weapons haven't fired in years," he said, "but I hear what you're saying — an admirable attitude."

The man found the pirate hard to read. He couldn't tell whether he was lying, telling the truth, or merely playing with him before slaughtering them all.

"Unlike yours," said the man. "There's blood on your hands, pirate; we've all read about you."

"There's blood on everyone's hands, my friend," he replied coarsely. "It's whether you choose to wash it off or not that counts."

The man's face remained stern. Mousebeard could see beads of sweat running down his cheeks.

"Sir!" called the other man as he appeared once more from the tower. "Lugwidge will open the storeroom doors."

Mousebeard looked to the man on the quay for an explanation. He pointed up to the bridge overhead.

"The storeroom up there," he said. "They'll send down a cage for you — and only you."

"That suits me," said the pirate. "And you can stand there and watch the ship for me while I'm gone...."

"I was going to do just that," replied the man.

"Good. I wouldn't want you doing anything useful," he growled.

⇒ ❋ ⇐

The cage shook as it lowered, descending at a fair pace until it came to a rest on the deck of the *Silver Shark*. Mousebeard stepped in and secured the door behind him. Once he was safely inside, it started to rise again, and his eyes followed the thick chain that pulled it skyward. Just meters from its destination, however, it ground to a halt.

"You won't try anything stupid, will you?" asked an old bearded man, leaning half out of the hole under the walkway. "We've had no trouble here for years...."

Mousebeard found it strange to see the professor again: his serious face was covered in lines and wrinkles, and his balding head even more hairless than before. When he spoke, his words sounded muffled, as though he owned false teeth, and his bright blue eyes were now yellowing and tired. Professor Lugwidge had been only a young teacher when he'd first met him, so the difference was all the more noticeable — he still wore the same earthy colored, well-cut clothes, though, and in particular a plain brown waistcoat.

"I'll not cause you trouble, Professor Lugwidge…"

Lugwidge was thrown by his words.

"Professor? No one calls me that here…."

"My name's Jonathan…Jonathan Harworth. Remember me?"

"You…," he said, returning his hand to the crank, which had halted the cage's progress.

"You were the friend of Isiah Lovelock — but I thought you'd died long ago…*you're* Mousebeard?"

He released the stop and turned the crank once more; the cage lifted into the box-filled storeroom and stopped with a loud clunk as it locked into place. Professor Lugwidge's eyes traveled all over the pirate, trying desperately to find a feature he recognized.

"It's time we had a little talk, Professor," said Mousebeard.

"It is?" he replied, quite dumbfounded. He opened the cage warily. "But I've heard such bad things about you…; I don't remember a young Jonathan ever doing any harm.…"

Lugwidge beckoned him along a thin corridor and into a cluttered room, filled with books and odd pieces of furniture. Two old Brown Mice sat atop a shelf and squeaked when they saw them.

"I would have thought you'd know better than most not to trust any news that came out of Old Town these days," said Mousebeard.

"Oh, but we're so far removed from all that. We can't get the *Mousing Times* out here, so we don't get much news; it seems to be only the worst, most gruesome stories that are capable of traveling along the wind to us. We're pretty much self-sufficient out here on the Murals, so we don't care too much."

The professor walked to a stove and placed a thick-bottomed kettle on to boil.

"Tea?" he asked. Mousebeard nodded in reply.

"But why have you come here? Surely you realize our aldermen will have alerted someone to your presence. Despite our position out here in the sea, we do still have contacts on the mainland.…"

"I'm sure someone has," Mousebeard replied, "but it's nothing we can't deal with. They wouldn't get here for days, so we have a little time."

He cut to the chase. "Are you still in contact with Isiah Lovelock?"

Lugwidge pulled up a seat and sat down.

"I'm afraid I'm not. That man has little time for the likes of me these days. And all those hours I gave up to his dogged learning of evolutionary history!"

"So you won't have heard about the Golden Mice?"

"Now there you're very much wrong—I think the whole world must know about them."

"He's a law unto himself," mumbled the pirate.

"Ahh," said Lugwidge, "but that's exactly what everyone thinks of you...."

"Yes, so I've heard."

"But there's more to your visit than just this, surely," said the professor.

Mousebeard gently teased apart his beard and withdrew the Methuselah Mouse, which immediately started to shiver. Lugwidge took off his glasses and swapped them for a thicker, more powerful pair. His pupils grew to double their size through the lenses, and he leaned forward to see the animal up close. After blowing warm air over his fingers, he delicately touched its back with his fingertips.

"You remember what you told us, all those years ago...," said Mousebeard.

"Ah...Porphyria Hokeline," he said quietly.

"What..."

Mousebeard pulled the mouse away.

"What did you say?"

The professor leaned back and wiped his brow.

"That was her name...the woman on Stormcloud Island," he said. "And I've seen this little fellow before. I met them both on a sailing ship as I was returning from an overseas expedition. She showed me the Methuselah Mouse, but she wouldn't tell me much about it—in fact I thought she was quite mad. All she wanted to talk about was where she'd been. The fact that I'd just seen the Tork Mice of Emben in their natural habitat didn't even register."

Mousebeard growled, and his fingers squeezed his kneecap.

"She cursed me...," he said, his voice serious and grim.

"Cursed you?" said Lugwidge, his nose wrinkling, lifting up his glasses. "Don't be silly…; I mean, she was odd, but…"

Mousebeard's face darkened, and Lugwidge suddenly started to fear him once more.

"Isiah also suffers it. She cursed us so that we may never meet again—I am cursed to forever roam the sea, Isiah trapped upon the land. I think she saw something in us, feared what we were capable of together—she'd have been kinder to kill me there and then.…That woman turned me into what I am now, and all because of this mouse I hold in my hand. And you may hold the key to it all."

Lugwidge jumped up and hastily prepared two cups for their drinks.

"I don't see what I can do to help you," he said uneasily. "I really don't know anything more. Like I said, I thought she was one Stinkle Mouse short of a bad smell."

"There must be something," said Mousebeard. "Think…"

"She was quite unhinged," he said, passing a cup to Mousebeard. "I mean, she seemed to think that she had just returned from *that* place, *that* mythical land of the mouse people…what was it called? We used to teach about it in Mousing Myths and Mouselore…."

Professor Lugwidge scratched his head.

"Oh, come on, Jonathan, you must remember...," he said, his eyes screwed tight and his fingers massaging his head, "where the Mussarians are supposed to have come from!"

"You don't mean Norgammon?" said Mousebeard.

"That's the one! That's the place! I told you she wasn't all there!"

A loud whistling noise surrounded the room, taking Mousebeard by surprise.

"It's just the wind," said Lugwidge; "you get used to that."

Mousebeard stood up and looked through the windows. Blue-backed Flying Mice were playing with the wind, letting its current lift them into the sky before folding their wings and plummeting to the sea. The windmill sails continued to turn steadily, and the clouds in the distance raced across the horizon.

"Norgammon?" said Mousebeard once more.

"Yes, I'm sure that's right. I mean it's just preposterous, isn't it?" replied Lugwidge. "And when I heard that, I tried to keep my distance from her—you never know what these folk might do in the cramped interior of a ship."

"But no one's been there, ever. It's not even thought to exist, really, is it?" muttered Mousebeard.

"Exactly!"

Mousebeard opened the window and let the strong wind blow in, ruffling his beard.

"I think you should turn your attention away from this woman, Jonathan. I can't see the cure to your curse being anything to do with her."

"You don't understand, Professor. She's the only link I have to the curse. I need to find out more about her."

"I'm sure you'll find out what you need soon enough, Jonathan," said Lugwidge, taking a sip of his tea. "These matters have a habit of solving themselves, but sometimes it just takes time — maybe even years."

Mousebeard pulled at his jacket and felt resigned to his fate.

"But Lovelock is growing more powerful by the day. His dominance in both the mousing and political communities is overwhelming. I fear that soon not even I might have the ability to stop him. I fear the one thing I don't have is time."

# The Bangarian Monk Mouse

THE GENTLEST AND SWEETEST MOUSE IN EXISTENCE, THE BANGARIAN *Monk Mouse likes nothing better than resting its head on its paws as though in prayer. A dark grey color, the Bangarian Monk Mouse emanates from the small island of Bangaria, where it peacefully coexists with the island's population of priests. This is one of the easiest mice to keep, due to its minimal food requirements, disregard for comfortable bedding, and need for a particularly small cage.*

### MOUSING NOTES:

*The Bangarian Monk Mouse enjoys plenty of peace and quiet, so keep the noise down.*

# The Getaway

KEEP HOLDING THAT LEVER UP!" SHOUTED ALGERNON, whose leather hat was now fully secured under his chin. In testing times it was always possible to tell Algernon's mood by the state of his hat: the more secure it was, the more concerned he was.

Scratcher felt his legs wobble beneath him as the submarine dragged to the left with the current and came to rest against the seabed.

"I didn't know they had submarines," he said, watching beams of light drift through the murky waters of Hamlyn's harbor.

"No, nor me," Algernon replied angrily, flicking an

array of switches that sent the sub's interior into darkness. "They must have found all the plans from my workshop....Blast! I knew I should have destroyed everything."

He swiveled his pilot's chair back around to the window and stared out through his wide glasses. Without his Boffin Mice to help, he needed six hands to work everything. But the probing lights of the enemy submarines hadn't spotted them yet, and as far as he was concerned, that was how it should remain.

"We sit here and wait," he said, clutching the gearstick with both hands. "If they spot us, you have to pull that lever down as fast as possible....You understand?"

"Got it!" said Scratcher. "But how are we going to rescue Emiline and Drewshank if we're stuck down here?"

"Young Scratcher, in times like this — as infuriating as it must seem — we have to look after ourselves first. Without the submarine, there'll be no escape for any of us!"

"I understand," he said sadly, "but if they do get away, how will they contact us? We're not in the right place anymore!"

"Hmph!" grumbled Algernon. He was truly stumped.

"And we won't be able to surface on the hour, like you'd planned."

"No…"

Algernon scratched his chin and immediately had a brainwave.

"Aha! We might not be able to surface, but one thing we can do…"

He jumped up and pulled a cord above his head. With a soft clunk, a metal box with handles sticking out from its sides descended from the roof. He pulled it down to his eye level and gazed into it.

"The periscope! I shall raise it on the hour to keep watch. How does that suit you?"

Scratcher smiled.

"That will be perfect," he said.

❧ ✳ ❧

The door to the Mouse Trading Center opened quietly and Indigo peered out into the evening gloom. A light mist was thickening in the air, spreading the glow of the oil lamps like ink blots on paper. He saw four soldiers lining the wall at the front and turned to Drewshank and Emiline.

"We're into curfew now, so there's no way out of this safely. As soon as they see us, the alarm will sound and everyone will be after us. You're sure of your friend and his submarine?"

"If Scratcher has done his bit, then he'll be with Algernon, and they'll be looking out for us every hour," said Drewshank.

"Here goes then...," said Indigo, placing his mousebox on the floor. He lifted the lid, and the Sharpclaws scrambled out, as alert as ever. Indigo pointed out the guards, and the mice ran off. They showed no mercy and attacked their victims with such speed and agility that the men didn't know what had hit them. Their weapons were sliced into pieces, and they ran off without a second thought.

"Come on!" whispered Indigo, as he made his move. He didn't stop to pick up his mice, but they were already following him as his feet hit the hard, cobblestoned street. Emiline was left speechless by how well trained his mice were.

The street led directly to the harbor, and they skirted around the boundary wall and skipped down the steps to the quayside. Within just a few moments they heard Lady Pettifogger shouting from behind them. The soldiers from inside the Trading Center were clustered around her and blowing whistles to alert the Old Town Guard.

"Where did Algernon say he'd be?" asked Emiline breathlessly.

"Over there," said Drewshank, continuing along the water's edge. The only ships that were docked were navy vessels, and he watched them nervously for signs of life. He stopped when he reached a small wooden shelter and saw the light was on. He looked nervously into the doorway.

"Can't stop," announced Drewshank happily.

Mildred snapped out of his dream and blinked sleepily.

"Mr. Drewshank? Is that you?" he said, his head spinning woozily. "Shan't say a word…"

Drewshank carried on, his spirits lifted by the sight of the Weather Teller. He followed the curve of the docks and eventually found the spot.

"Here it is," he proclaimed to himself, noting the thick metal chain falling into the water, and taking deep breaths to steady his heart.

Indigo's mice finally reached his side, and he picked them up and secured them in his mousebox.

"So where is it?" he asked, staring into the gloom. Emiline caught up with them and couldn't see the submarine either.

"Well, if I had an idea of the time," muttered Drewshank. "Oh, hang on!"

He ran back to the shelter and peered inside at Mildred, who was asleep once more, his stick propped up on the side of a chair and the dead fish on its end rolled into a ball. On the moldy wall sat a crooked wood-framed timepiece.

"Ten to nine," he said quietly, as a loud gunshot fired out in the distance. "Which means ten long minutes to be captured! Gah!"

He ran back, fighting the urge in his legs to slow down.

"Ten minutes till the hour!" he said, leaning over to combat a sharp stitch that was sitting in his ribs.

"Ten minutes!" snapped Indigo angrily. "The armed guard is out now—we won't last that long!"

"Algernon won't let us down, I know it," said Emiline

earnestly. She ran out along a wooden wharf, feeling the mist grow thicker around her. The sea was dark and choppy beneath her feet, and she looked down into it, waiting for a sign. A gunshot rang out once more and she heard something fall into the sea with a soft plop. Her heart started to race.

⇒ ✳ ⇐

Algernon dragged the periscope to his eyes and stared into its murky black viewfinder.

"Keep a watch out that window, lad!" he said, waiting for the periscope to break the water level.

The other submarines were still searching for them, but without any light coming from Algernon's sub it was like looking for a needle in a haystack. Time and time again Scratcher's hands were tempted to pull the lever, but he managed to remain calm.

"Anything?" he asked.

"Nothing," replied Algernon, "and there's a mist picking up!"

Suddenly a small object flew downward past the window.

"What was that?" said Scratcher.

"Eh?"

Another came shooting downward.

"Look!" Scratcher pleaded, as a chiming ring sounded on the side of the submarine.

Algernon released the periscope and swiveled his chair to flick a line of switches. The inside of the sub became bathed in blue light, and Algernon readied the controls.

"They're bullets!" he said frantically. "Pull that lever, boy! Something's happening!"

Scratcher jumped to attention and pulled downward. The submarine's engine started to roar, and Algernon shunted the gearstick forward. With a slight shudder, the craft zipped forward and rose to the surface.

➤ ✳ ◄

Emiline was crouching on the wooden planks with her hands covering her head. Shots were coming from all sides, and the Old Town Guard had cut them off from the quayside. Drewshank and Indigo were kneeling beside her, weapons in hand, but their only protection against the soldiers' rifles was the mist.

"It's gone past the hour now," said Indigo. "Where are they?"

"They'll be here, I know it!" said Emiline.

Drewshank squeezed his fingers tighter around his sword's grip.

"They will," he said, as a wave broke against the wharf and splashed over him.

"The soldiers are coming," said Indigo, feeling the wooden planks rock with the increased weight of the men.

Emiline looked into the black water again. All sorts of thoughts ran through her mind as she stared aimlessly. But then, like a moment of inspiration, a white light shone out of the water and right into her face. The wooden planks beneath her splintered and crunched, and Algernon's submarine appeared from below—barging its way to the surface before squeezing through the wooden posts to the other side.

"They're here!" she cried happily.

The submarine slowed to a halt and the small hatch on its back flipped open.

"What are you waiting for?" asked Scratcher, leaning

out and offering his hand to his friends. The wooden jetty started to wobble, and Emiline jumped off, landing on the metal top of the submarine.

"What took you so long!" she said hurriedly before falling inside.

"Where's Spires?" asked Scratcher, noticing his absence.

Indigo jumped next, and he acknowledged the boy before descending.

"He didn't make it," said Drewshank, landing on the sub and falling in.

"What?" said Scratcher, pulling the lid down to seal the submarine. Bullets hit the metal, but they did no harm as the submarine vanished into the water.

"Where is he?" he asked, pulling himself into the now cramped interior.

"Horatio?" said Algernon, unable to take his eyes off the controls.

Emiline stepped forward and caringly placed her hand on Algernon's back.

"They killed him," she said, feeling her stomach tumble inside.

"What!" he shouted, spinning his chair around. He instantly turned back to the window and kicked his foot down.

"They what?" said Scratcher.

"They killed him," said Drewshank plainly.

Scratcher's face grew pale.

Algernon twisted a valve, and the submarine started to growl as the engines worked harder. He pulled his goggles down over his glasses and focused on the route ahead.

"They will pay dearly for this…," he said coldly.

# The Boater Mouse

A FAIRLY RARE BROWN MOUSE, FOUND ONLY IN WARMER CLIMATES, THE *Boater is rather unusual in its method of travel. Instead of crawling across land, like most mice, the Boater likes to hollow out branches or large seeds in order to form small raft-like vehicles that float on water. Blessed with unusually large ears that double as sails, the Boater Mouse harnesses the wind like no other. It also has a peculiar ability for direction: the species has been known to sail almost 150 miles in its search for a mate, and neither sea nor ocean can hold it back.*

### MOUSING NOTES

*This isn't the easiest of mice to keep, as you are legally bound to offer it a home with either a lake or large pond. Under no circumstances can it be caged.*

# A New Adventure

THE CAGE CARRIED EMILINE, SCRATCHER, AND INDIGO upward, their stomachs turning over as they watched the *Silver Shark* fall away from them. Algernon's submarine was once again securely lashed to the deck, and the daylight reflected off its copper surface.

"One more pull!" shouted Fenwick from above, as the walkway emerged over their heads. His rotund mouse, Trumper, scurried up onto his shoulder to watch them emerge through the floor.

With a slight crunch, the cage slipped into place, locked tight, and the door swung open—much to everyone's relief.

"That's so far up!" exclaimed Scratcher. "My legs are like jelly."

"Come on in," said Fenwick, smiling, and ushered them through the storeroom to a vaulted meeting room, whose floor pitched at a slight angle. Algernon, Drewshank, and Mousebeard were sitting with Professor Lugwidge around a dark wooden table. Oil lamps lit the room from above and highlighted their faces in such a way that made them look even more serious and grave than they were.

"Meet Professor Rudolph Lugwidge," said Algernon to the new arrivals, "and everyone else meet Indigo."

Everyone said hello, but none felt that they could say anything more. The atmosphere was too tense for niceties. Mousebeard was visibly fuming, his eyebrows leaning down so heavily that his eyes were almost covered.

"I've been told of our loss," said Mousebeard, "but I wanted to hear it from you, Emiline."

Emiline suddenly felt nervous and exposed. At the pirate's command she took a seat and started recalling the events at Hamlyn. Emiline watched his eyes, and as she struggled to describe the butler dying, she noticed them grow distant and sad. She realized that Algernon's and the pirate's loss was even greater than her own. Her mouth felt dry and her throat became sore, so she stopped talking.

Portly ran down Emiline's shoulder to her hand, where he immediately wrapped his damaged tail around her finger.

Mousebeard took a breath so deep it was as though he hadn't inhaled for days.

"I still can't believe that the message was a forgery," said Algernon. "It looked so much like his writing."

"And we have nothing of his," said Mousebeard. "No word of what it was he died for?"

"Nothing," said Drewshank, noticing Emiline's difficulty and coming to the rescue. "They'd cleaned out the whole room."

"Then they have truly hit us hard."

Mousebeard let out a rumbling growl as he smashed his fist into his opposite palm.

"I only have this," said Emiline quietly, remembering the bloodstained handkerchief and removing it from her pocket. She placed it on the table. "He was holding it so tightly...."

"Just like Horatio," said Algernon, allowing a smile to escape from his otherwise stern face. "He's stitched his name onto it!"

Mousebeard looked at the bloody cloth and saw the

delicately stitched lettering in the corner. His beard bristled, and his eyebrows rose to reveal his dark eyes once more.

"And since when did Horatio's name start with the letter 'N'?" he said curiously, picking it up between his thick fingers and holding it to the light. "How are your eyes these days, Algernon?"

Mousebeard spelled out the letters as he scanned along:

"N, O, R…"

He stopped dead and looked to Lugwidge.

"…G, A, M, M, O, N."

"My word!" said the professor.

"Norgammon?" said Drewshank quizzically, unaware of its meaning.

Algernon pulled the leather hat from his head for the first time in weeks and held his scalp.

The pirate turned the handkerchief onto its side and read aloud a set of coordinates stitched in tiny letters and numerals along its edge.

"I can't believe I didn't look at it," said Emiline, kicking herself.

"And so things come full circle," said Mousebeard. "Maybe that woman wasn't quite so mad as you thought, Professor. This is too much of a coincidence!"

"A coincidence?" said Algernon.

"The professor, here, explained to me that the woman on Stormcloud Island claimed to have found Norgammon," said Mousebeard. "And now Lovelock seems to have discovered its location."

"Hang on," said Drewshank; "you've lost me! What's this Norgammon?"

Lugwidge shifted his spectacles on his nose and looked at the handkerchief.

"Captain Drewshank," he said, his old teaching instinct coming to the fore. "Norgammon is an ancient, lost land from a past so distant to us now it's been considered a myth for centuries."

"Could it really have existed?" asked Algernon.

"Well," said Lugwidge, scratching his chin, "our mousing mythologies must originate from somewhere, I suppose. But I find it hard to believe it...."

"Our mythologies?" asked Drewshank.

Professor Lugwidge peered at the captain over the top of his glasses.

"Ancient mythology tells us only a small amount concerning Norgammon, but it is an intriguing tale. If I remember correctly—and it's a long time since I taught ancient mousing lore—the people of Norgammon, the Mussarians, were renowned for worshipping mice as though they were gods."

"That sounds daft," said Scratcher.

"You might think so now, but back in the distant past, they didn't have our science and understanding to explain the ways of the world. To them, everything that occurred was directly related to the well-being of mice. There were gods of the sea; gods of the air; gods of the mountains...the list goes on—and all of them were mice."

"So why haven't I heard of this Norgammon or the Mussarians before?" asked Drewshank.

"You clearly didn't study hard enough at school," said the professor sharply. "It's thought that a great apocalypse destroyed their civilization. You find whispers of its culture in ancient history books; there are a few stories and tales. The Mussarians are thought to have been a warrior race, and a quite brutal one too, but the facts are very murky indeed. I mean, that Norgammon has escaped our searching for so long would say to me that it doesn't exist anymore—if it ever existed in the first place. It's quite likely the creation of someone's overactive imagination."

"But stranger things have happened, Professor," said Algernon. "Remember when that girl found the Deep Sea Lava Mouse? That creature was thought to have been extinct for nearly a million years—the only record of it in fossils—and yet there it was, caught in a fishing net...."

"That is a fair point," said Lugwidge, "although a matter of the Deep rather than our more visible world above the sea."

"But this is not just about the past," said Mousebeard forcefully. "That Lovelock is interested in it would say to me there's more here than meets the eye. Maybe the key to breaking my curse lies there?"

"Now that would be going too far, and being too presumptuous," said Lugwidge.

Algernon rubbed his forehead excitedly.

"But just consider, leaving the curse aside for a second,

what might be discovered in this ancient world?" he said. "It would be the archaeological and mousing find of the century!"

"And Lovelock will waste no time in taking it for his own," said Mousebeard.

"Beatrice Pettifogger did mention that Lord Battersby was off exploring," said Drewshank. "Perhaps the search is already under way?"

Mousebeard banged his hand down on the table, and all of them jumped in their seats.

"It could be another Golden Mice fiasco all over again," said Algernon. "And just look at what he's done with those!"

"What do you mean?" said Mousebeard.

"In Hamlyn," replied Drewshank. "I had the misfortune of being witness to one of their new breeds."

"New breeds?" said the professor.

"They've successfully crossed the Golden Mouse to create a much larger hybrid—they intend to farm it for its golden fur."

"Heavens...you are lying!" said Lugwidge.

"No sir," said Indigo. "I was the mousekeeper there.

They finally bred a workable hybrid nearly two months ago."

"Workable!" exclaimed Drewshank, before baring his teeth and tapping them with his fingers. "It tried to savage me!"

"Indigo has some tales to tell of the place," said Emiline. "You should see his trained Sharpclaws!"

"Sharpclaws?" exclaimed everyone.

"And his boot!" added Emiline. "He has a secret compartment with super-charged mousing explosive and all sorts in it!"

Scratcher sat quietly, feeling a little dismayed. Emiline had hardly spoken to him since they'd met up in the submarine. She seemed to find Indigo much more interesting.

"And these Golden Mice, where are they now?" said Mousebeard.

"They've been sent all around the Great Sea," said Indigo. "There are factories everywhere—they have them all set up and ready. I swear they're probably already harvesting pure gold by the bucketload."

"Then matters are worse than even I feared," said

Mousebeard. He looked to Algernon, who instinctively knew what he was about to say.

"Our old acquaintances, Algernon. We need to contact them. Our daggers need to be drawn...."

"I know," he replied. "Professor Lugwidge, do you have an Onloko Mouse in need of some action?"

"We have a collection of the finest — it's a necessity out here," said Lugwidge. "I'm sure there might be one kicking its heels."

"Wonderful," he said. "You don't charge, do you?"

Lugwidge laughed at him.

"You can have this one on me," he said.

"So with that all settled," said Mousebeard determinedly, "we now need to plot our course to Norgammon, if it's there to be found. And if we can ruin Lovelock's plans in the process, so be it."

"It would appear we're at the start of yet another adventure," said Algernon, smiling. "And, Professor, will you join us?"

Lugwidge shook his head.

"Oh no," he said. "These legs aren't what they used to be. Besides, you lot haven't changed — here you go, off on a wild mouse chase. I hope this time you don't get more than you bargained for."

"This time," said Mousebeard, "we'll be prepared!"

⇒ ✳ ⇐

"There are ships on the horizon, Captain!" came the word from below.

Mousebeard looked out of Lugwidge's window and noticed four ships — currently just black specks against the overcast sky — far out in the distance. The rest of the crew were already on board the *Silver Shark*, and the submarine had been hoisted onto its deck. The pirate picked up his hat and made his farewell.

"Thank you for your help, Professor. I must be leaving," he said, buttoning his jacket. It was far looser these days.

Professor Lugwidge shook his hand and smiled.

"No matter what else occurs, and no matter what you've done in the past, I'm proud of you, Jonathan. If I can ever provide more help…"

Mousebeard interrupted.

"I think you'll soon have soldiers knocking on your door. You'll have enough worries of your own.…"

"Ah, soldiers…," said Lugwidge, "nothing I can't handle. Besides, it's far too easy to distance yourself from the world when action is required. I'm happy to have played a role!"

Mousebeard's huge hand clamped over the professor's shoulder.

"And it won't be forgotten," he said.

He left the room and walked to the supply cage that was ready and waiting for him. He closed the door behind him, and as Professor Lugwidge released the winch, letting the cage drop, Mousebeard saluted.

"You should never have quit at Old Rodents'," he shouted.

Professor Lugwidge craned his head through the trapdoor.

"I didn't! I was made to leave!"

"*Fired?*"

"Could say that!"

Mousebeard laughed, and the cage hit the deck of the *Silver Shark*. He walked out and called to his crew as Lugwidge disappeared from view.

"Hoist the sails, raise the anchor! What are you all waiting for?"

"Aye, sir!" shouted everyone.

With a level of excitement amongst the crew that hadn't been felt for weeks, the *Silver Shark* pulled away with the wind in its sails. Norgammon lay in wait somewhere out on the Seventeen Seas, and they were determined to find it before the Old Town Guard.

# The Balletic Tree Mouse

FOUND ONLY ON THE ISLAND OF ANKON THOR, THE BALLETIC TREE MOUSE *is difficult to spot in the wild, where it inhabits only the highest treetops. It's a real treat to find, however, as this mouse is a born entertainer: to win its mate, the male of the species will undertake amazing gymnastic feats while hanging from the branches by its tail. Due to the risky nature of this bizarre mating ritual, this mouse is more often seen lying dead on the forest floor than it is alive.*

MOUSING REGULATIONS:

*An easy mouse to cater to, but branches or hanging bars are a must within its accommodation. If you wish to keep this mouse alive, a very soft bedding or flooring is also desirable.*

# Across the Barren Sea

EMILINE SAT IN MOUSEBEARD'S CABIN STUDYING *The Great Ages of Mice* by Samuel Moleridge. She was consumed by its stories of mice and humans and was only now realizing that the creatures had been cherished for hundreds of years. The rain had eased ever since the *Silver Shark* had passed through tropical waters on its way south, and it had seen its fair share of sunny days and windless nights as it crossed the Great Sea, heading farther than even Mousebeard had ever gone before.

Despite its capabilities, though, it could still never travel quite fast enough for Emiline. She'd spent a lot of her time in the company of the pirate, who'd agreed to teach her the finer art of mousehunting, although his patience regularly waned after half an hour's tuition. Among his many lessons, Mousebeard's advice on how to trap a flying mouse with just your bare hands proved the most exciting — and also the most costly. Two Messenger Mice failed to return after a series of botched attempts, but it was all seen as useful experience.

As usual, Portly was always nearby. He lay asleep either under her hair or beside her hand most of the time — and his tail proved to be a useful bookmark if Emiline ever needed one. She'd worked steadily from left to right along the pirate's bookshelves, reading book after book just to pass the time. *The Great Ages of Mice* had given her the best insight into the lost world of Norgammon, and it contained many weird and wonderful descriptions written about the land throughout the ages. But, just as Professor Lugwidge had said, all the accounts said something different, and there was little solid information amongst its pages.

Emiline read page after page, looking at the peculiar artistic representations of Norgammon. She laughed out loud when she saw that one of them showed mice walking upright on two legs, and when Scratcher appeared at the door she was still wiping tears from her eyes.

"You still in here?" he said.

"I am indeed," said Emiline.

"Want to help with the Watcher Mice? I think there's a problem with some of them, could be a bit of a cold, or something."

Emiline shook her head.

"I'm happy here, at the moment," she said. "Maybe later?"

"Oh, okay."

Scratcher stood for a moment staring at her.

"Can I help you look at the books?" he said finally.

"I'm fine, thanks," said Emiline, smiling. "Portly here's already enough help, even when his tail gets in the way."

"I might go and ask Algernon for some ideas then," he said quietly. "I'll see you when you're done."

Emiline turned the page of the book and looked back to where Scratcher had just been. She realized that he was probably quite lonely, but there was plenty for him to occupy himself with if he put his mind to it.

The sun shone through the small windows of the cabin, and Emiline listened to the wind crack the sails into shape. Their speed was picking up—if only it could go even faster, she thought. Two months at sea was already far too long....

⇒ ✳ ⇐

"Algernon," said Scratcher, swinging down into the gun deck.

Algernon had taken up residence on the lower deck and was fiddling with a wrench and some bolts.

"The Watcher Mice aren't well, and I can't think what it is."

"How very interesting!" said Algernon, raising his eyebrow at the same time as lifting the wrench into the air. He tapped it a few times on his head.

"I'd say quarantine them for a short while, see what happens..."

"I've already done that," replied Scratcher. "They're safe and far away from the other working mice. But they just seem down and lacking energy."

"Don't we all!" proclaimed Algernon. "But I suppose they have been at sea for a while now, haven't they?"

"Yeah, I guess..."

"Maybe they're pining for home — they do like to have a run around on the grass occasionally, don't they?"

"They do," said Scratcher.

Algernon stood up and walked to him. He looked him up and down and patted him on the arm in a friendly manner.

"Are you all right?" he asked. "I haven't seen you with Emiline of late."

"I'm fine," he said, lying. "She's always busy reading, or learning how to hunt mice with that Indigo."

"Ah!" said Algernon wisely. "So that's it…"

"Eh? That's *what*, exactly?"

"Oh nothing," he replied. "Say, do you want to help me down here for a bit? I could teach you all about Sonic Orientation."

"Sonic what?" he asked.

"It's something I'm working on for my submarine. I've been thinking about how the squeak of the Giant Whale Mouse can travel so far underwater, and I thought there might be a way of harnessing it, either for long-distance communication or even detection. If you didn't know, sound bounces around under the sea like nobody's business—just like it does above ground. I thought it might be a way of detecting those blasted new submarines of the Old Town Guard. Next time I see one, I'll give it what for, I can tell you!"

Scratcher laughed.

"I'd love to help you," he said. "Just let me take another look at these mice, and I'll be right back!"

≫ ✳ ≪

Drewshank marched over the deck and found Fenwick remonstrating with a sailor. Fenwick's mouse, Trumper, was happily perched on his shoulder, rubbing its head against its owner's neck.

"What's this all about?" said Drewshank sternly, placing his hands at his hips.

"We've spotted Tacking Mice far out over the starboard side," replied Fenwick. "And I'm trying to persuade old Scubbins here that we need to get more Watcher Mice out on deck! We can't keep sight of them alone."

"That would seem logical," said Drewshank. "Tacking Mice can, after all, knock the ship into all sorts of shapes!"

"Aye, sir," said the sailor, "but young Scratcher's said we're short of them. They've come down with a bout of sickness."

"Well, Scubbins," said Drewshank, "let's ask Indigo to

help—he'll have keen eyes, I'm sure. Have you seen him lately?"

"With Emiline, Captain," said Fenwick. "They're playing with them blasted Sharpclaw Mice or something. I still ain't happy about having them creatures on board."

"They helped us escape, man! Go easy on the poor mice."

Fenwick laughed.

"Poor mice! Captain, you've gone batty. Their claws are sharper than razor blades!"

"Ha! That may be so, but they're great in a fight. I'll get Indigo to help you; I'm sure he won't mind."

"Aye, sir," said Fenwick, and he placed his hand at his neck and stroked his mouse. Its belly wobbled a little, and a foul smell escaped into the air.

"Ooh," said Scubbins, his face turning green, "get your mouse in order, Fenwick!"

⇒ ✳ ⇐

"Take hold of that," said Indigo.

Emiline secured the thin rope between her fingers, her eyes never straying from the round piece of wood attached to its end.

"This was a trick I learned long ago," he added. "It takes a special kind of wood for this to work—a root of the Bilbab tree—but you'll soon see how helpful it is."

He looked around to check that the deck was momentarily free of sailors and, opening his mousebox carefully, he released a Sharpclaw. The mouse dropped down and stood still but for its massive claws tapping at the floor.

"Sharpclaws like to be teased," he said. "Pull the rope—gently at first."

Emiline tugged at the cord, and the wooden disc skated across the deck. The Sharpclaw's eye was taken. It struck down with a claw, aiming for the piece of wood, but missing.

"Now pull again…"

Emiline stepped backward and pulled the cord once more. The Sharpclaw leapt at the wooden disc and sliced downward with its paw. As its claws hit the target, Emiline realized the qualities of the wood. The mouse's claws stuck firm. It growled, but no matter what it did, it couldn't free itself.

"Now just raise the rope up a little…."

Emiline lifted it, and the Sharpclaw's paw rose into the air helplessly—its claws remained trapped.

"That's miraculous," said Emiline, amazed. The mouse was caught, good and proper, as the wood clung to its claws like marmalade to a wasp.

Indigo picked up his Sharpclaw and apologized to it. He took some water, dripped it onto the wooden disc, and, as it became saturated and expanded, the mouse's claws came loose.

"Just keep the wood dry," said Indigo, "and there's no Sharpclaw it can't catch."

"The Bilbab tree?" said Emiline.

"That's the one..."

"Did I hear Bilbab mentioned?" asked Mousebeard, appearing behind Emiline like a storm cloud over the horizon. Drewshank followed close behind and stood watching them all.

Indigo got up and placed his mouse back in its box.

"Just a trick I learned, sir," he said.

"I don't mean to stop you," said Mousebeard, his arms clamped behind his back. "I'm impressed by your knowledge."

The pirate continued walking along the deck, his eyes watching the boy.

"You'd do well to listen to him, Emiline," he said.

"I know," she replied; "this Bilbab wood's amazing...."

"Where did you get it?" asked Drewshank, stepping forward.

"It grows natively on an island far from here—I forget its name now—but I picked this piece up in a market on Hamlyn."

"Very interesting," said Drewshank, losing interest quickly. "I wondered if you wouldn't mind helping Fenwick for a while?"

"Sure," he said. "I bet Emiline's got plenty to do of her own, anyway."

She shrugged in reply.

"He just needs someone to watch out for Tacking Mice. Apparently our Watcher Mice are sick."

"I can do that," said Indigo.

"You'll find him at the bow," said Drewshank.

Indigo wasted no time and set off to the other end of the ship.

"So what's he like?" asked Drewshank. "He seems quite knowledgeable for his age."

Emiline blushed slightly.

"He is," she said. "He knows a lot about mice—much more than me...."

Drewshank smiled at her.

"He's a useful guy to have around, that's for sure."

"I think so...," she said.

Emiline pulled at her mousebox.

"Do we have far to go?" she asked, as a group of sailors ran past and started climbing the ropes with Rigger Mice clinging to their backs.

"Funnily enough," said Drewshank, "we should be there within a few weeks—if it exists, of course. If it doesn't, then our supplies are running short and we might find ourselves in a tricky spot!"

"We'll find it," she said. "Mr. Spires knew what he was doing. He knew how important these coordinates are."

"I hope you're right, Emiline, I really do."

⇒ ✳ ⇐

"So the red wire goes here?" asked Scratcher, his hand speckled with burns from a misdirected soldering iron.

"That's right, then hold it down firmly..."

Algernon helped him finish the joint and made him

sit back while he lifted up the machine's cover. He slid the fascia down over the mass of wires, and eventually it clicked into place with three switches bared at the bottom. In its entirety, the machine was a metal cube, about half a meter wide. It had a knob on the left-hand side, a covered wooden dome at its base, and a blank glass screen on its front.

"Now then, Scratcher," said Algernon, brimming with excitement. "I'll let you switch it on!"

Scratcher wasn't sure if being asked to turn on the machine was an honor or a death sentence. He hesitantly directed his index finger toward the metal box.

"If you insist…," he said.

As he pressed the left button, a strange glow shivered behind the small glass screen on the fascia.

"Perfect! Perfect!" said Algernon, jumping up and down. "And the next!"

Scratcher tried to smile, knowing things were likely to get worse, and pushed in the next button. The machine started to buzz.

"Is that meant to happen?" he said, as the noise grew louder and louder.

"Yes, yes!" replied Algernon. He twisted the knob on the side of the machine, and the noise lowered to a mere hum.

"Much better," muttered Algernon. "Now the last!"

Scratcher jabbed the third button, and suddenly the entire gun deck started to hum and throb. Screws and bolts began creaking and popping up out of the floorboards, and the vibrations grew unbearable. Scratcher's ears started to hurt, and he quickly jabbed the button to switch it off again.

Algernon stood looking perplexed.

"That wasn't meant to happen, then?" asked Scratcher sarcastically.

"Umm, no. I hadn't planned for that," he said. "The screen should have definitely picked something up after that!"

"You mean that you expected that noise?"

"Oh yes, well, something similar to that, yes!"

Scratcher blew out a sorry sigh.

"Don't worry, I'll sort it," said Algernon, switching all the buttons off. "Must just be a faulty connection — yes, that's all it can be."

"So will you help me?" asked Scratcher, trying to change the subject.

"The mice? No, I'm not sure what's going on there...."

"No, I meant the other things — that I asked you about a while ago. You said you'd help me with my own inventions too!"

"Ah, I remember, of course I did. Yes, pass me those small cans, and we shall be on our way!"

⇒ ✳ ⇐

Indigo was standing on a short ladder at the bow, his eyes glued to the crests of waves rippling off the starboard side of the *Silver Shark*. Tacking Mice were breaking the water, zigzagging across the sea in tight formation, and they drew ever nearer. To the untrained eye, Tacking Mice are a beautiful distraction — their silvery-grey fur sparkles in the water as they dart left to right and back again through the waves — but any sailor worth his salt knows they have the ability to hammer a hull to smithereens. Their rigid, streamlined bodies can act like battering rams when they're powering at full speed, so it's always best to keep clear of them — if you can.

"Captain Mousebeard!" shouted Indigo. "They're almost on us! Starboard side!"

"How many?" shouted Mousebeard.

"About eight, and increasing by the second!"

"Hard to port!" ordered the pirate.

The ship swung around awkwardly, and all of their legs were pulled away from them.

"Decoys!" shouted Fenwick, rushing to Mousebeard's side. "We need a decoy!"

"Good thinking," replied the pirate, his big boots firmly planted on the ground.

"We could use the launch," said Drewshank, hurrying out of Mousebeard's cabin. "Set it adrift?"

He stepped up to look over the ship's side and caught sight of the Tacking Mice breaching the water, intent on reaching the *Silver Shark*.

"They're gaining on us!" he shouted.

"Hard to starboard!" called Mousebeard.

The pirate knew that playing the mice at their own game was the only way to buy time. The ship lurched back into their path, and they darted away, soon to return.

"The launch it is!" said the pirate. "Load it with cannonballs, then lower it over the side — and make it fast!"

Sailors soon appeared, weighed down with cannonballs,

and they loaded up the small boat that sat on deck. It was a sad but worthy fate for the launch, and as Drewshank unbolted the armored sides of the ship, Fenwick dragged it across to send it to its doom.

"I've got it steady, sir," said Fenwick, lowering the boat to the sea with some stout ropes. "When you're ready!"

Indigo watched the mice surge closer; they were within meters when he gave the call.

"Let it go, Captain!" he shouted.

"Drop it!" bellowed Mousebeard.

The boat hit the waves at a fair speed, weighed down by the weight in its hull. It skipped over the water before slowing gently.

"Here they come!" said Indigo.

Suddenly the Tacking Mice veered out of the water and smashed into the small boat's side. They hit it so hard that the wood splintered and cracked. Again and again they disappeared beneath the water, only to return with more venom and speed.

"Keep us on course!" shouted Mousebeard, watching the distance between the mice and them grow by the second. "They've taken the bait!"

Drewshank walked to Fenwick and surveyed the wreck of the launch from the opened side. The mice's attention was fully taken by the little vessel, and as it finally sank to the bottom of the sea, they seemed satisfied and swam away in the opposite direction.

"As if they didn't know we were here!" said Fenwick happily.

"Good work!" said Mousebeard, approaching Indigo. "You sailed much before?"

"A little," he replied, stepping down from the ladder.

"You've got a good knowledge of these things," said the pirate inquisitively. "Where'd you learn them?"

"I didn't go to school," he said. "I was lucky—I had a tutor."

"Anyone I've heard of?"

"Maybe..."

Indigo waited a short while before answering.

"You heard of Arlo Jones?" he said finally.

"Who hasn't?" said Mousebeard. "I read the *Mousing Times* whenever I can find a copy. He's always in it—one of the best hunters in the land. He can sniff out a mouse at a hundred paces."

"Yeah, I was lucky—like I said."

"And we're lucky to have you with us, Indigo," said Mousebeard. "Someone of your caliber…good to have you on our side."

"Thanks," said Indigo. "It's nice to be on board—I've heard a lot of stories about you…."

Mousebeard clasped the boy's shoulder and squeezed tight.

"You'll have a few stories of your own to tell about me now, then," he replied, and a wide grin crossed his beard.

⇒ ✳ ⇐

Mousebeard awoke to the sound of Fenwick banging at the door to his quarters. His hammock twisted as he slid from it, and with a thud his feet hit the floor. Mousebeard had a habit of sleeping in his boots.

"There's something strange goin' on, sir!" said Fenwick, as Mousebeard appeared before him.

"What?"

"The sky, sir…"

Mousebeard picked up his hat and pulled it tight down over his head. He looked upward, his eyes drawn to peculiar ribbons of colored light twisting their way across the heavens.

"What time is it?" he asked, rubbing his chin through his beard.

"Early morning, sir."

"Are we still on course?"

"Aye, sir. The mice never lie."

Two Night-light Mice scampered past, the beams of light from their eyes passing over Fenwick's legs.

"And how close are we to Norgammon?"

"The captain…sorry, Mr. Drewshank reckons we're near—a week's sailing at the most."

Mousebeard walked to the ship's side and lifted himself up to get a look at the sea. The wind was whipping up the glassy, impenetrable water into choppy peaks, highlighted by the strange colors in the sky.

"I've seen this before, Mr. Fenwick," he said.

"You have?"

"A long time ago I sailed far south of Midena, and the days became much shorter, with just a few hours of light. The sun barely rose above the land. We saw these other-worldly lights twice on that voyage, and none of us could forget them. Some people thought they were the souls of sailors lost at sea, warning of treacherous conditions ahead."

Fenwick found himself thinking of shipwrecks and squalls.

"What do you think?" said Drewshank, approaching with Scratcher at his side.

"Let's just keep our course, and we'll see what comes our way," said Mousebeard.

"So what happened on that voyage?" asked Fenwick.

"I encountered my first pod of Icefall Mice...."

"The ones with those long spiraling tusks?" said Scratcher.

"That's them," said Mousebeard.

"And what happened?"

Mousebeard smiled and gripped Fenwick's arm.

"They took a great chunk out of the front of the ship...."

Fenwick's face turned to horror.

"But these things make you better sailors!" said the pirate. "We'll reach our destination, I assure you!"

# The Icefall Mouse

THE ICEFALL MOUSE IS A LARGE DEEP-SEA MOUSE, RENOWNED THE WORLD over for its long tusks that protrude from the sides of its mouth. These mice are found in icy waters near the Southern Pole, and they live in pods of up to fifteen. Icefall Mice have particularly poor eyesight and can cause great damage to ships when rising to the surface for air or when hunting. Unfortunately, because of this they are best avoided despite being one of the most graceful creatures in existence.

MOUSING NOTES

Too large for aquariums, these mice are not suitable for collections.

# The Gateway to Norgammon

W HEN THE SUN ROSE THE NEXT MORNING, MOUSEBEARD surveyed his maps and called for a detailed position to be taken. It revealed that they were so near their destination as to be almost on top of it.

"We're almost there, then," said Algernon, who was standing beside Mousebeard in his cabin.

Drewshank walked in with Emiline and Scratcher and explained that the wind had eased, but they were concerned at their direction.

"If it's going to be around here, we'll see it soon, won't we?" said Drewshank hopefully.

"We'd better," replied Mousebeard. "Our water rations are running low."

"I have an idea, Jonathan," said Algernon, referring to Mousebeard by his real name. "I've been working on this machine..."

Scratcher groaned.

"It utilizes whale sound," he added. "I think it might be able to help us find it, if it's there to be found."

"And if it works..." said Scratcher.

"Have faith, please," said Algernon.

"It can't hurt trying," said Drewshank.

"Your machines usually have some benefit," said Mousebeard. "It won't explode, though, like that mouse dryer you made? I still have nightmares about those poor Puff-tailed Mice."

"I'll bring it up onto the deck, and we can find out!" he said.

Everyone walked out of the cabin with trepidation. A new machine of Algernon's was always an exciting moment, and when he returned with the metal box, an air of anticipation rippled through the ship. He placed it down on the floor and pressed the first button. The screen on the front of the box flickered to life.

"A good start!" he exclaimed, pressing in the second button.

A loud hum grew out of the machine, and Algernon watched the screen attentively as he twisted the knob on the side.

"Close your ears," said Scratcher ominously, as Algernon pressed the third button. "If it's anything like last time, they'll be bleeding soon."

Suddenly, the hum turned into a low-pitched buzz, and the deck shook. Everyone's feet started to tingle. Algernon quickly twisted the knob again, and the buzz turned to a high-pitched squeal before dying away completely. As the ringing in everyone's ears eased, a huge smile grew on Algernon's face. It was being lit by the green light from the screen, and his eyes were focused on a large yellow blob at its top. He twisted the knob once more; the buzz sounded again and then died away, and his smile remained.

"I don't believe it!" said Algernon.

"Did it work?" asked Drewshank.

Mousebeard peered down at Algernon and the screen in

front of him. Algernon pointed to the yellow shape that was glowing on the screen.

"I think we've found Norgammon," he said exultantly. "I think we've got it!"

"That blob?" said Mousebeard.

"That's it! If my judgments are correct, we're about a day away, full sail. That's it, I'm sure!"

"So what are we waiting for?" said Drewshank. "Let's get a move on!"

⇒ ✳ ⇐

The first sign of Norgammon was a clump of low-lying clouds drifting on the horizon. Ever since he'd seen the yellow shape appear on his machine, Algernon had been glued to the spot, but for bathroom breaks and dinner. Over the course of the day, the strange shape had moved steadily down the screen of his machine until it was almost at the bottom. It was only a matter of time before the lookout called out from above, and as he did so, a massive cheer whipped around the ship. Mousebeard felt his hopes rise in an instant.

The pirate stood at the helm and watched as the clouds

drifted across to reveal Norgammon itself. He looked through his telescope and tried to understand what he was seeing. A massive black wall, which must have reached nearly a mile into the sky, grew out of the sea. There was no break along its length, which soon rose to fill the whole horizon.

"It's the most peculiar thing," said Drewshank.

Mousebeard passed him his telescope.

"There's a small island in front of it, straight ahead," he said. "We should aim to land there!"

Drewshank lifted the telescope to his eye. In front of the wall, poking out of the sea, was a low, rocky outcrop, whose crumbling black mass was falling apart. The remains of a castle, with little in the way of walls or battlements left to speak of, sat precariously on top. At its farthest side, a narrow, sloping causeway ran across the water, with foaming white breakers crashing at its rocky base. From humble beginnings, just a few meters above sea level, it rose higher and higher like a mountain path, winding in serpentine fashion until it reached the wall about a quarter of the way up its side.

"That path leads to a huge gate...," said Drewshank,

pointing the telescope higher. Housed in an archway that wouldn't have looked out of place in a grand cathedral, a pair of iron doors sat at the end of the path.

"It's a strange place, all right," said Mousebeard. "We should be able to draw close enough to that causeway safely....Without our launch, things will be a little tricky, but our hull should withstand a few scrapes."

"I'll pass on the word!" said Drewshank. "Norgammon, here we come!"

He called to Fenwick, and soon the orders were flying around the ship.

The *Silver Shark* slowed to a snail's pace and drew closer to the island. The first thing that struck them about it were the colonies of sea mice. There were Long-nosed and Yellow-belly Mice resting in the sun, and most prominent of all were the Saggy-necked Silt Mice, who performed airborne acrobatics as they dived into the sea seeking their next meal. They provided color to an otherwise very black rock, born of volcanic blood.

"Drop the sails!" shouted Mousebeard.

Without the wind's aid, the ship floated along on its own momentum until its port side was a stone's throw from the causeway. A cluster of menacing-looking rocks reared their heads as the swell died down, and Mouse-beard ordered for the anchor to be lowered into the sea. Once the ship had slowed to a halt, Drewshank measured the situation by opening the ship's armored gangplanks and peering over the side.

"We'll need to be in tighter than that to get across safely," he said.

The ship sat a few meters off land, and no one in their right mind would have risked the jump.

"Captain!" said Indigo, pacing along the deck. "I'm a strong swimmer—I can climb up the rocks with a rope. I'm sure I could find a place to tie it so we can pull in closer."

"Sounds like a fine plan," said Drewshank. "Fetch me a rope!"

Indigo removed his jacket and mousing belt and laid them down on the deck.

"Aren't you taking off your shirt as well?" asked Drew-shank. "You'll ruin it!"

Indigo shook his head and set about removing his boots.

Fenwick passed him a rope, and the boy tied it around his waist. Taking a deep breath, he leapt headfirst off the starboard side and disappeared briefly beneath the waves. He reappeared at the foot of the black outcrop, his body revealed with the movement of the rolling sea. His hands grasped the rocks like claws, his fingers rigidly holding tight.

"Good man!" shouted Mousebeard, impressed with his agility.

Indigo scrambled up the sloping cliff and soon reached the top. With his clothes sagging and dripping, and water flowing down the small of his back from his ponytail, he looked around for a secure piece of stonework. He found the remains of the lower half of a narrow window, pushed it a few times, and finally assured himself it would do. With a sturdy looped knot, the rope was tied firm, and he gave Fenwick the signal.

"Ease up the anchor!" said Fenwick. "Let us drift!"

As the ship gently ebbed back out to sea, the rope grew tighter, and three sailors took the strain, using the anchor winch to pull the ship back in tighter to the rocks.

"Excellent work, men!" shouted Drewshank, as the gap narrowed further, and with a running leap he jumped onto the causeway. There was only a meter between the ship and the land now, and with a few planks of wood they'd soon have a safe bridge onto dry land.

More sailors leapt across with further ropes, and in a few minutes the ship was firmly secured and lined up along the path. It made an ideal quayside, running flat for a few hundred meters before climbing the long ascent to meet the wall.

"So we made it," said Drewshank, passing Indigo his things. "Norgammon…"

"It's so vast," said Indigo. The wall dominated every-thing around, and its thick black blocks—each of them bigger than the *Silver Shark*—were joined seamlessly, with-out a sliver of light between their edges.

Algernon jumped onto the land, followed by Emiline and Scratcher, and he walked along the causeway to where it joined the outcrop. He ran up its gently slop-ing side and came upon the rundown castle. The outlying ruined walls were all that remained. They were a meter thick in some places, although apart from a few remaining bat-tlements, their height barely rose above his head. The walls were covered in a mixture of vines and mouse droppings, and the whole area smelled rotten. He kicked the dirt and realized the ground bore marks of where rooms once stood, with grassy lumps and hollows now in their place.

"It looks really old," said Scratcher, shooing away a gang of Yellow-belly Mice that had sneaked up on them to see what they were up to.

"Doesn't it just...," he replied. "And look at what's left of the stonework—it all fits together like a perfect puzzle!"

Algernon removed a notebook from his pocket and drew a few lines while making notes of the mice that inhabited the outcrop.

"What are you doing?" asked Emiline.

"Always carry a notebook and pen!" he said. "Always! You never know what you might forget."

He continued drawing as Emiline wandered off to talk to Indigo. He was standing quite still, letting the sun beat down on his wet clothes.

"That was a great dive," she said, placing her hands in her jacket pockets. Portly appeared from under her hair and watched the sailors rush back and forth behind.

"Thanks," he replied coolly. He squeezed his hair, and a stream of water trickled down his hand.

"You've made quite an impression on ship," she said.

Scratcher watched them from afar and decided not to approach.

"Just trying to help," said Indigo.

"I can see," said Emiline.

"Hey!" shouted Drewshank from the *Silver Shark*. "Let's get together everything we need! No time to waste!"

"It should be an interesting ride," said Indigo.

Emiline agreed. "I've not had a dull moment since I met Captain Drewshank."

The sun vanished behind the immense wall as it passed over the highest point in the sky, and a shadow flew over the ship, sending the temperature much lower.

Mousebeard stood on deck contemplating their discovery. He stroked his beard, and his fingers brushed over the Methuselah Mouse, which was awake and scratching its back. He had no idea what might lie ahead. For so long he'd pushed the curse to one side, almost to the point of forgetting about it. But here he was, with more reason than ever to be hopeful that answers were within his grasp—even if he could do little about it for himself.

"Quite a find!" shouted Algernon, skipping back down onto the causeway with a spring in his step. He leapt back onto the ship.

"Indeed," replied the pirate, "but I've never felt so useless!"

"Oh come on now, Jonathan. Drewshank loves doing all this stuff. He loves to be important and in charge again."

Mousebeard's huge laugh boomed out, causing everyone to stare at him.

"Aye, he'd make a good captain one day!"

"Wouldn't he just!" said Algernon, picking up a few useful items and shoving them in his pockets. "Say, do you think the Old Town Guard will catch up with us soon?"

"Of course they will. They'll be stronger and in greater numbers, but they'll be no more determined."

"On those points I'd agree. But when we leave you, keep checking my machine. It seems to be working for the moment, and you should be able to pick up if a ship's approaching."

"And I'll use my old seadog eyes too," the pirate replied.

"Algernon!" called Drewshank, who was about to leave the *Silver Shark*. "You ready?"

Algernon waved in reply.

"Find the cure to this curse ...," said Mousebeard.

"If it's there to find," replied Algernon, in high spirits. "I'll not return without it!"

He jumped from the deck onto the causeway and bumped into Scratcher. He wasn't his cheerful self; instead he was kicking his heels.

"Do we have enough food?" said the boy.

Algernon caught sight of Fenwick, who was laden with supplies.

"I believe there's plenty in those bags to keep us all for a week," he said.

"Judging by this weight around my shoulder," said Drewshank, joining them, "I'd say two...."

"So we're all ready?" asked Emiline, as she approached with Indigo.

"Yes, we are," said Drewshank.

"Any news," boomed Mousebeard, "and I want to know!"

"We shall return as soon as we find anything!" promised Drewshank.

With that they set off up the long winding path. It narrowed as it grew steeper, and its length seemed never-ending as it rose higher and higher. The breeze turned into a gale as they neared the wall, and all soon became careful in their footing—the cliffs on either side of the path plunged straight into the sea, and a wrong step would end in almost certain death against the rocks and boulders at the cliffs' base.

They continued ever onward: the wall's stones looked more massive and inconceivable as the climbers approached and, gradually, the path leveled out into a wider platform. They were so far up now that the *Silver Shark* became but a silver minnow upon the sea, and just a short distance in front was the ledge that held the gateway.

Fenwick reached the entrance first, and he leaned backward, looking upward at the sheer scale of its construction.

"Iron doors!" he said, slightly overwhelmed. "Not much left of 'em!"

Algernon saw for himself the massive rusted iron doors

that hung open: three imposing bolts lay on the floor, their brackets fallen to pieces through age. Their panels had long suffered the attack of the salty sea winds and were as ravaged as a moth-eaten old woolen sweater. He reached out and pushed one of the red-tinged, crusty squares that formed the door, and it crumbled in his hands.

Emiline took the initiative and squeezed through the gap between the doors to enter the long, dark tunnel. She could see a distant white circle at its far end, and she realized exactly how thick the wall was.

"It goes on forever!" she said, her words echoing into the void.

Drewshank pried the doors farther apart and found that most of their metal tumbled to the floor in pieces no thicker than paper.

"After you, then!" he said. He touched the walls of the tunnel — they were damp, moldy, and freezing cold — and he instantly had to rub off the slime that had gathered on his fingers.

Emiline found that the urge to run was too strong, and she looked back at her friends briefly before heading off into the new world.

# The Shaggy Night Mouse

ENDOWED WITH AN INCREDIBLY LONG AUBURN COAT THAT IS THE ENVY OF *all Bald Spotted Mice, the Shaggy Night Mouse is a nocturnal and distinctly shy creature. Its presence in an area is more often noticed by the discovery of its discarded fur than by a sighting of the mouse itself. In certain parts of the world, this mouse is bred for its fine hair, which can be harvested yearly with little discomfort to the animal. The hair can be used for many things, from paintbrushes to fine scarves, and it has also been put to good use in men's wigs.*

MOUSING NOTES:

*This mouse is suited to collectors with special night facilities. They take very little looking after, but their hairs do get everywhere.*

THE GREAT PYRAMID

MOUSE STATUE

OUTPOST RUINS

GATES OF NORGAMMON

CASTLE RUINS

Norgammon

# The New World of Old

EMILINE WALKED OUT INTO THE DAYLIGHT AND GASPED in awe. From the roaring sea they'd left behind, she'd arrived in a world so lush and green, and so vast and unbelievable, that her breath was stolen from her. She was standing far above the ancient land—the tunnel had brought her out onto a wide viewing platform that was at least a hundred meters above the treetops—and it took her a moment to find her bearings. The wall towered above her still, its height only diminished occasionally by the light clouds scudding over its top, but it raced away for miles on either side until it was just a faint line on the horizon. A gentle wind blew her hair to the side, its blond strands fluttering like flags in a breeze, and she moved closer to the edge to soak it all in.

Across the vast carpet of forest directly below her, three strange, stepped golden pyramids stood tall in the distance. They sat in a triangular formation, the largest at the back, in the center, while the two smaller structures sat at either side like a pair of Halfung Hunting Mice at their master's feet. Their three peaks dominated the forest, but rising even higher behind them was a series of rolling hills: a soft mist ebbed over their tops, drifting down into the forest like heavy candle smoke.

Emiline looked closer into the trees and spotted the remains of stone towers and buildings teetering amongst trunks and branches; she could see the sparkling of water—a shimmering river flowed through the land, its presence only visible in patches where the trees were thinner. She could smell the sweet scent of fruit and flowers, mingled with the musky aroma of decaying wood carried on the breeze.

"It's so beautiful, isn't it," she said to Portly, who had ventured onto her shoulder. His ears were erect and his nose twitched in the air.

"Oh my," declared Drewshank, walking into the open with a sword in his hand. He wasn't usually one for crying, but his right eye started to twinge at the beauty before him.

One by one, the rest of the group arrived behind Emiline, and all of their faces held the same expression of astonishment.

"Look at the trees!" said Scratcher, pointing to a large specimen with blood-colored leaves.

"And the pyramids!" gushed Algernon, taking off his glasses in the hope of seeing farther.

Indigo crept to the right of the platform and crouched down.

"And the mice…," he said quietly.

Taking great care so as not to alarm it, he approached a tiny mouse that was no larger than his thumb. Its ears were far bigger than its body, and its eyes blacker than black. The mouse casually started to clean itself, and Indigo held his palm out steadily in front of it. Without any concern, the mouse scampered calmly onto his hand.

"It's not at all scared of me," he said, quite astonished. "I've never known a wild mouse like it."

"Could I have a look, Indigo?" asked Algernon.

Algernon pulled the small notebook from his jacket and made Indigo hold the mouse in front of him. He slid a pencil from the notebook's spine, opened a clean page, and started to draw.

"I don't know if there's time for that," said Drewshank, shaking his head. Indigo was already carrying an expression of exasperation.

"Just a second," said Algernon, finishing the rough sketch and jotting a few notes by its side. "Might never see it again—got to make as many studies as possible."

"Captain," said Fenwick, walking to the left side of the platform. He'd spotted the long flight of crooked, rainworn steps that ran down to the ground, and took a few paces down.

"So there's our path!" said Algernon, rubbing his hands with glee. "Who's up for a bit of exploring?"

≫ ✳ ≪

The party started the long walk to the ground. Each step sagged in the middle like an old pillow, and without a handrail—a massive oversight, thought Algernon—it was a treacherous passage. Hand in hand they clambered down, before eventually reaching the damp forest floor. As soon as they'd entered the shadow of the trees, the wonders of Norgammon appeared before them.

The forest was so calm and peaceful, and even Algernon's normally excitable temperament was stayed by what greeted them. He looked into every mousehole and into every tree at the new sights and couldn't remember ever feeling so humbled: it was as though no human had ever been there, such was the purity of nature before them. Occasional mouse noises filled the air, some squeaks loud, others raspy and low.

Emiline walked deeper into the forest and pushed her hand against a grey tree trunk whose bark was so old and crusty it crumbled with her touch. With a flutter of leaves, a mouse flew down from the branches above her head and stopped dead in front of her, its small wings flapping so fast that they were just a blur. It hovered as it stared at her, sniffing her nose and her face, and then it suddenly shot off to grip a nearby tree trunk. Emiline almost lost sight of it against the wood — its body was much smaller than a Messenger Mouse's, and its chalky brown and grey mottled fur looked so similar to the tree bark that it could have been camouflage.

"Did you see that?" said Emiline, captivated by the mouse. She realized it was a new species, or at least a species that had been lost for centuries.

"Keep still, everyone!" said Algernon. "Let me get a good look!"

He made a slight shuffle forward, trying to get closer, just as another mouse leapt up out of the undergrowth. It jumped through the air so quickly that he only caught a glimpse of its short black fur. Its mouth snapped open, and with a bite that crunched as it closed, it caught the winged mouse in one swift action and pulled it to the ground.

"You got Portly safe there?" said Indigo, creeping forward with a gleeful smile on his face.

Emiline placed her hand to her shoulder and was relieved to find he was still with her. He squeaked at her touch.

"A jumping meat-eater?" whispered Algernon. "What a find!"

Drewshank looked down to his feet as a swarm of bright white mice came scurrying past, their ears upright and alert. They were so small he dared not move in case he stood on them. The mice rushed along with leaves and twigs in their mouths, as though they had very serious business to attend to.

"Don't move!" he said, watching the mice navigate the ground till they reached the safety of a spiky bush.

"This place is crawling with mice!" said Fenwick, feeling a blob of liquid land on his bald head. He looked up and saw a peculiar mouse with eight legs, hanging from a branch by a long white thread. It had just thrown down a ball of spittle in a pathetic attempt to catch him in its sticky gloop. Fenwick lifted his hand and tugged the mouse's thread, and the creature dropped into his hands. He stared at it in total wonderment.

In the way it might take your eyes a few seconds to adjust to the dark, it was the same when viewing the creatures in the forest. Everywhere they looked they could see mice, and not one was in *The Mousehunter's Almanac*.

"This is all very lovely, but I think we should make camp," said Drewshank, spoiling the moment somewhat.

"Find ourselves somewhere safe to spend the night and plan our next move. I bet at least one of these lovely mice has sharp venomous teeth it would like to sink into me."

"Captain," said Emiline, "I saw a ruined building from the platform. It wasn't that far from here."

"That sounds ideal," said Fenwick. "Which way?"

Emiline looked into the forest and then turned back to her friends.

"This way!" she said with a small amount of certainty, pointing in the right direction, and marched off.

➤ ✳ ⬅

They walked for about an hour before Emiline saw the ruined building. It was more of a treehouse than a townhouse, as a huge tree had taken root in its foundations and now wore the walls like an ill-fitting corset: its trunk and branches broke free through the upper floor and burst out of the long-fallen ceiling, so there was little space left between its sandstone walls. Rubble was strewn over the floor, both inside and out, and the uneven, broken stone staircase led only to a thick branch covered with round yellow leaves.

The ruin stood alone in the forest and looked more like an outpost than part of any town. It must once have been a tall structure, and there were many broken pillars lying entangled with roots and tree trunks around its edges.

"I don't know if I'd buy it," said Drewshank, "but it's certainly got potential."

Indigo trod carefully around its walls. He poked his head through a glassless window.

"It looks ideal," he said, kicking a stone to check its sturdiness. "Someone can keep watch in the branches, while others rest down below."

"Well remembered, Emiline," said Algernon. He took out his sketchbook and quickly drew some of the carvings that remained on the building's stonework.

"Right," said Fenwick. "Let's get settled and make some grub—I'm starving."

"I might go wandering first," said Algernon. "And I'll bring some wood on the way back!"

"I'll join you," said Scratcher.

The pair left the rest to settle in, and Emiline climbed the tree to join Indigo high up in the branches.

"Want some of this?" he said, passing a stubby piece of

dried meat to Emiline. She took it and started to chew. It tasted sweet and smoky, but bits kept getting stuck in her teeth.

"It seems too tranquil out here; something makes me think we've had too easy a ride so far," Indigo said.

"Sitting up here reminds me of keeping watch in the crow's nest," she said, gazing through the treetops at the pyramids in the distance. "I always wanted to get out of Old Town, but I never imagined I'd find myself traveling halfway around the world. . . ."

Indigo smiled and tore into a piece of meat with his teeth.

"Sometimes it seems that fate has things lined up for you, doesn't it," he said.

"I don't believe in fate," said Emiline. "You can change your future if you try hard enough. It's just about trying, that's all."

"Maybe that's right," he replied.

Emiline listened to the warbling sound of a mouse calling out from the treetops.

"Where are you from, Indigo?" she said earnestly, realizing that she'd never even thought to ask him.

"I was born a long way from Midena," he said. "I doubt you'll have heard of it."

"Try me."

Indigo scratched his neck, smiling at Emiline's insistence.

"I'm from an island called Urla, on the outer edges of the Great Sea. But I left there when I was young. I don't remember the place now...."

"I'd lived in Old Town all my life before setting out with Captain Drewshank," said Emiline.

"It was always my intention to go to Old Town," revealed Indigo, "but I got a bit caught up in Hamlyn...."

"Didn't we all!" said Emiline.

"Yeah, they've certainly ruined that place," he grumbled. "But you've done well for yourself — as much as I wouldn't tell it to his face, Drewshank's a great captain...; and Mousebeard, well, he's another story entirely. How come you ended up with such a pirate?"

"It was a bit of an adventure that went awry, really," she explained. "Scratcher and I — we sort of stuck it out and ended up on the baddies' side."

"You know, I get the feeling Scratcher doesn't like me much," said Indigo. "He tries desperately not to talk to me."

"He's being a bit weird lately," said Emiline, "but he's all right."

"I think it's because he likes you, and you're often with me."

Emiline gave him an amazed stare.

"Don't be silly," she replied hastily. "That's Scratcher!"

"And?"

"Well, why would he act weird because he likes me?"

Indigo let his mice out of their mousebox. They scampered along the branch and casually scraped their long claws across the bark to clean them.

"Because he's a boy," he said knowingly. "He's jealous...."

Emiline frowned and hunched her shoulders.

"Whatever you say," she said.

⇒ ✳ ⇐

Algernon found a patch of bare earth and sat down to scribble a few more pictures in his notebook.

"Sit down, Scratcher," he said, finding the boy's continuous pacing around a tree frustrating.

"I can't settle," said Scratcher. "I don't know what it is."

He was about to walk to Algernon, when he caught his foot in a hole. He tripped and fell straight to the floor, his hand hitting the ground first.

"You all right?" asked Algernon. He got up and walked over to the boy before attempting to lift him to his feet.

"I'm fine," he said.

Algernon pulled Scratcher's hand, but with the added force on the ground, the soil beneath them started to give way.

"Algernon?" said Scratcher with surprise. The soil crumbled rapidly, and his lower half slid down into a hole. He could feel his feet dangling.

"Where are you going? Hold on!" said Algernon. He pulled harder at the boy's arm, but suddenly the floor collapsed beneath him too, and they fell straight down into a dark hole about two meters deep.

Algernon landed with a bump.

"Blow me down!" he said, rubbing his backside.

Scratcher looked around him as the soil stopped crumbling. The sides of the hole were dotted with tiny tunnels, all intermingled with roots breaking through the soil like wizened fingers. He looked again, and suddenly the holes were filled with hundreds of eyes, all glowing brightly.

"Would you look at that!" said Algernon. "Tunneling mice!"

"They must have overcooked the number of tunnels," said Scratcher, perking up a little.

"My thoughts exactly," added Algernon. "They'd weakened the ground to the point of breaking. And look at their miner's-lamp eyes! What a lovely blue glow they give off!"

The mice stayed in the tunnels and didn't allow the travelers to get a decent look at them. All they could see were little noses twitching in silhouette.

"I don't think they're very happy with us," said Scratcher, chuckling.

Algernon let out a laugh and started to clamber up the sides of the hole, clutching some roots to help himself up. Once he'd reached the top, he leaned over to help his friend.

"Shall we head back now?" asked Scratcher, dragging his feet out of the hole.

"I must say, my stomach's grumbling like a Moaner Mouse," said Algernon. "A bit of food would fix that right away."

"I'd die for a bit of pie," said Scratcher, looking above him; the sun was setting, and a beautiful red glow was spreading over the sky.

⇒ ✳ ⇐

As dusk turned to evening, the wonders of Norgammon were still enchanting everyone. Emiline had found numerous colorful mouse droppings, which had made everyone laugh—particularly the blue ones. Algernon had been determined to store some to take back to the ship, but as strong as his will was, he couldn't argue with Scratcher's point that they might contain all sorts of new diseases that could harm the ship's mice.

They'd built a small fire, eaten some delicious food, and found themselves the center of attention when a group of waist-high mice with frizzy grey fur and small, beady eyes wandered into the ruin to warm up. Drewshank had been the least impressed with them, as they didn't smell very nice and had sat right next to him, but it was a moment that he'd certainly remember for a long time. And of course, it had been the perfect opportunity for storytelling.

"... And then the Mudflat Mouse said to the river," quipped Algernon, "you might be the strongest of them all, but you're still wet!"

Algernon couldn't contain himself. No one laughed, however, and he soon fell quiet.

"That was awful," said Drewshank, throwing a small chunk of wood onto the fire.

"I don't see you telling any jokes!" Algernon replied.

"I could tell you about the time I got stuck in a cave with a Buzzbat Mouse?" said Drewshank.

"Go on, then!"

"So it was between me and him — a battle to the death. You know how it is; Buzzbat Mice have those big stingy things on the end of their noses, and they charge at you, with every intention of finishing you off. But I was quick! I'd just had my hair cut, and I'd saved the trimmings in a small box in my pocket..."

"You did what?" exclaimed Algernon.

"Don't you all keep your cut hair?" said Drewshank.

A chorus of "No!" rang out from everyone around the fire.

"Anyway…as you may or may not know, the big eyes of the Buzzbats are particularly sensitive, so I thought on my feet—I mean, I had no weapons or anything, other than a piece of hard bread, and I really wanted to eat that. So I ended up throwing the locks of my hair out at the creature."

"And they got stuck in the mouse's eyes?" said Indigo.

"Didn't quite get that far," he said. "The mouse breathed them in as it charged at me, and collapsed in a sneezing fit. Did the trick, though, and gave me enough time to escape."

"Are you making this up?" asked Scratcher.

"I'd never dream of it," said Drewshank, much offended.

"I suppose it was slightly better than Algernon's joke," he said, not wholly believing himself.

Everyone sat silently as they considered Drewshank's story with bewilderment, and then Scratcher spoke up again.

"How about you, Indigo?" he said forcefully. "You

haven't said anything, and you must have billions of stories."

Indigo was seated upright with his hands joined around his knees, and he looked at Scratcher resentfully.

"I'm useless at stories," he said.

"Oh come on," said Drewshank. "Tell us something about Hamlyn, or even where you learned to train those Sharpclaws—that's pretty impressive...."

Indigo considered what he could say, and threw a twig into the fire and watched it shoot up in flames.

"I could tell you about my first Striped Sharpclaw...," he said reluctantly.

"Good man!" said Algernon.

"Perfect!" said Emiline.

Indigo continued. "To own a Sharpclaw is a pretty major deal where I come from—and it's something not everyone's able to do."

"Where *are* you from?" interrupted Drewshank.

"An island called Urla..."

"I'm still none the wiser," said Drewshank. "Carry on!"

"So you have to be of a certain age, with certain abilities," added Indigo. "It's a rite of passage, I suppose. As soon as you reach eight years old, you're sent on a hunting trip, along with two experienced mousehunters, and you have to capture your own Sharpclaw."

"At eight years old?" said Fenwick. "That's young to be doing that!"

"It's just how it's always been," replied Indigo. "As the sun sets, you're left alone in the forest with some water and a knife, and you do your best. It's up to you to find the means of trapping the mouse, and also to catch one."

"The Bilbab tree!" said Emiline.

"Finding that's the easy part—you get a bit muddy digging for the roots, but that's bearable. The hardest part is not being eaten by the Grime Mice that live in their branches. And so once that's accomplished, you head for the outer edges of the forest and wait. Striped Sharpclaws, in their natural habitat, rise just before dawn, so that's the best time to get them; they're usually a bit sleepy first thing and take the bait quicker. You have to be careful to find a loner, though—they're nasty if you get a few together."

"What happens if you don't catch one?" asked Drewshank.

"It's not the end of the world. But in order to become a soldier, you need a Striped Sharpclaw at your side — it's the rules — and to be in the army is considered the greatest accomplishment amongst my people."

"Why aren't you a soldier then?" asked Scratcher.

"I *was* a soldier," he replied.

"You were a soldier?" said Emiline.

"It's the only place to learn how to train Sharpclaws to a fighting standard. I thought it was a worthwhile thing to do."

"I'll say," said Drewshank. "I quite fancy having a pair of those myself!"

"I could teach you someday," said Indigo.

Drewshank thought about putting in the hours to learn another skill, and then realized he was fooling himself — he was good enough as he was.

"That's incredibly interesting, Indigo," said Algernon. "I should like to hear more about your land one day."

Indigo shrugged and held out his hands to warm them in the flames of the fire.

"It's really not that big a deal," he said.

"I think it is," said Emiline.

As Scratcher sighed and buttoned his jacket tighter, the group carried on talking about their greatest mousing achievements. They talked for hours, until the dead of night and the effect of long days at sea took their toll. As the night sky glittered with stars, and a quarter moon watched over them, they gradually all drifted to sleep—the kind brought about only by feeling safe and exhausted. The peace of Norgammon was enough to bring them contented dreams, but the tranquility wasn't to last.

➣ ✳ ➢

"Get up! Get up!" whispered Indigo, his hands shaking Emiline's shoulders.

Her eyes opened, and she saw that everyone else was in a state of shock after being woken in the same way.

"There are soldiers in the forest! Get your stuff and don't make a sound."

Fenwick threw dirt over the embers of the fire, trying to conceal any evidence of their presence.

"Have your weapons ready," he said. "I can see one!"

The group stood in the shadows of the ruined building, pressed hard against the crumbling walls as the first soldiers appeared through the trees in the far distance.

"There's another lot over here!" shouted one of the soldiers, pointing into the trees.

At the sound of a gunshot, the forest floor started rumbling. Emiline looked to Algernon, who looked to Drewshank, who in turn looked to Indigo. A flock of flying mice took off into the sky, emitting a screech of concerned squeaks. Leaves scattered everywhere.

"Ready, Rufus!" shouted another soldier. "Here they come!"

Emiline peeked over the wall and saw Scratcher doing the same next to her. They watched the forest as the rumbling turned into heavy thuds that grew increasingly loud as something massive approached. A second gunshot fired out; nearby trees buckled forward, and as their roots twisted upward to face the sky, a giant red mouse came charging through the forest. It cast aside the trees with its terrifyingly huge paws, uprooting them with ease. Emiline ducked back into cover. The mouse galloped on, passing the ruined building and missing it by barely a few meters. It was so huge that it was taller than the forest: its red eyes reflected the fear in its mind, its claws tearing into the undergrowth without concern for what might be in its way.

As the mouse passed, and the soldiers chased after it, two more giant mice followed in its wake. One jumped straight over the building in a daredevil leap that revealed its lighter white underside that was almost the size of the *Silver Shark*'s hull. Fenwick crawled out of the ruin and scrambled along the floor, looking back through the path that the mice had cleared. He turned in the other direction and watched the soldiers hurl roped harpoons at the creatures. The last of the giant mice reared up on its haunches as the barbed points clung to its dense fur and fatty flesh, the ropes growing taut as the animal pulled. It wailed with pain; the ropes had been tied to numerous trees, and the combined strength of them had stopped it in its tracks.

"Keep it tight!" ordered a ginger-haired soldier, running to the mouse with a rifle aimed at its head.

The creature's cries grew more intense. Its body swayed

above the canopy, claws flailing around and chopping down into the trees. The soldiers surrounded it and hurled even more harpoons into its flanks.

"Hold it there!" shouted the soldier. "I think we have it!"

The mouse snapped down with its enormous teeth, sweeping its jaws lower along the forest floor. With each snarling cry, the mouse lost strength; and it eventually slumped down to the ground, pulling three heavy trees down with it. All the soldiers cheered, and the ginger-haired man, who appeared to be in charge, prodded its mouth with the end of his gun.

"Nice work, men! Tie up its legs and get it ready for carriage. Lord Battersby will be pleased with your efforts."

"Battersby!" said Drewshank, diving forward and joining Fenwick. "So they're already here...."

# The Puff-tailed Mouse

ONE OF THE MORE DELICATE BREEDS OF MOUSE, THE PUFF-TAIL GETS ITS name from the white pompom-like growth of fur on the end of its tail. Each Puff-tailed Mouse pays great attention to its coat (and tail in particular), regularly cleaning and licking itself to maintain the soft, silky sheen that it is so famous for. Because of this, it is popular with the upper classes and can often be found nestling around the necks of well-to-do folk out for their afternoon constitutional.

### MOUSING NOTES

This mouse is a regular to mouse collections the world over, and many collectors pride themselves on securing the mouse with the largest puff on the end of its tail. The biggest puff ever recorded reached 14.3 centimeters across and was found on a mouse owned by Earnest Crumbly.

# The Hunt

IN THE SHADOW OF A ROUNDED RUINED BUILDING, WHOSE walls were covered with fine carvings and worn reliefs, Lord Battersby stood with his foot resting on the chest of a large, dead mouse. The man leaned proudly over his kill, twisting his curled mustache with the tips of his fingers.

"That'll be something to show them in the Old Town Gentlemen's Club!" he said boorishly.

"It looks just like the extinct Saber-tooth Mouse," said Lieutenant Smedley. "I wasn't expecting anything of that sort out here. We've managed to capture a live specimen too. Only one man got injured—lost an arm actually—but he'll have a great story to tell his family when he returns home!"

"That's the spirit, Smedley! This whole adventure is one that will go down in the history books as the greatest expedition of all time. If only we had greater space in the *Stonebreaker* for more cages. We could fill it twice over with all the new species we've discovered!"

"Lord Battersby!" called a young soldier. He appeared from the forest with a rifle in his hand: his thick ginger hair was brushed sideways and emphasized the whiteness of his face. "We've captured a giant mouse."

"That is good news," said Battersby, stepping down off his kill and addressing the soldier directly. "Locarno, isn't it?"

"Yes, sir."

"Ahh, Rufus Locarno—I fought with your father at the battle of Barnabus Ridge. He'll be thrilled to hear of how well you're doing."

"Thank you, sir. I fear the mouse might die of its wounds, though. It proved to be a hard catch!"

"Ahh, but that can't be helped, Rufus. Dead or alive, these creatures will still have the same impact in Old Town."

"Sir," said Lieutenant Smedley, "we should really try

and return with live mice...sir. The Mousing Federation won't look kindly on us if we kill too many."

"Smedley, I hear what you're saying, but when a life is at risk, the human must come first. Have you seen the paws on that creature? It could kill you with one swipe."

"Yes, sir, I've seen them."

"Just remember, Lieutenant, they're only mice. No matter what Isiah Lovelock might say, I have no time in the Old Town Guard for soldiers who place the life of a furry animal over that of a human. You agree?"

"Oh yes, sir, absolutely!"

"And, Rufus, what are your views on the matter?"

Rufus was surprised at being included in the conversation.

"Me, sir?"

"Of course! You know a thing or two about mice," said Battersby. "No matter how special or endangered these creatures are, we humans must come first, mustn't we?"

"I agree, sir," he replied.

"Good! You'd do well to listen to people like Rufus, Smedley. He's got his head firmly screwed on!"

"Definitely, sir," replied Smedley, his voice meek and distant.

"And while you're here, Smedley, is there any news of the pyramids?"

"Yes, sir. We've entered the two smaller ones, but we're still struggling with the Great Pyramid. It's totally sealed shut—we might have to use explosives."

"And what have you found?"

"There are plenty of wall paintings—murals of humans and mice seem to cover every wall. We've taken pictures and made extensive notes on their creation, texture, and so on. I must admit to being a little horrified by some of the mummified remains we've discovered, and there are also catacombs containing thousands of mouseskulls!"

"And, sir...," said Locarno hesitantly. Smedley gave him a look of total disapproval for interrupting his moment.

"... The mousekeeper has made great progress on identifying those mice depicted around the base of the Great Pyramid. She's proved to be quite talented in that area, and if all those mice are still alive and not extinct, she thinks we may have only half of those shown."

"Truly?" said Battersby. "There could really be twice as many new species out here as we've trapped?"

"Yes, sir," he said. "This place really is a lost world of mice. It's better than we could ever have hoped!"

"Then that spurs me on! Smedley, let's blast our way into the large pyramid, and we'll see where it gets us."

"I'll set to it immediately, sir."

⇒ ✳ ⇐

Drewshank crawled back into the ruin and sat up against the tree trunk.

"So the Old Town Guard got here first," he said.

"They'll outnumber us ten to one," said Fenwick. "And as much as Mousebeard wants us to look around, we can't risk our lives here!"

Algernon took his leather hat from his pocket and strapped it securely around his head.

"We should return and warn Mousebeard. He's a sitting duck out there — and also our only means of getting home."

Drewshank realized their dilemma. He buttoned the

collar of his jacket so that it covered his neck right up to his chin.

"Maybe we should…," he said.

"But we can't just run away!" said Emiline. "Not now. We've come so far."

"I don't know," said Drewshank. "I just can't risk it."

"Why don't I follow them," suggested Indigo. "At least find out what they're up to. As I've seen for myself, the Old Town Guard is always up to something."

"I can't let you go by yourself," said Drewshank sternly.

"I have my mice," he replied. "They'll look after me."

"I'll go with you!" said Emiline.

"And I will," announced Scratcher.

"Now this is silly," said Algernon. "We might as well all go at this rate and be done with it."

Drewshank made his authority known.

"I can't send you young mousekeepers out there into the unknown," he said. "Not after what happened last time."

"But we've been through so much!" said Emiline. "We're quite capable of dealing with things…."

"No, I insist you go back to the ship," said Drewshank.

"I shall go and find out what I can, and, Indigo, maybe if you'd join me?"

"I'd relish the chance," said Indigo.

Emiline started to fume.

"That's not fair," she said.

"Emiline, that's enough!" said Algernon.

"But…!"

"Emiline!" said Fenwick angrily. "Do as he says!"

After a few moments of awkward silence, the deal was done.

"If there's any trouble," said Drewshank, "if any of us get split up, then we meet back here! Agreed?"

Everyone agreed, and with a flurry of parting hand-shakes the two groups went their separate ways.

Lord Battersby walked across the stone plaza that sat in front of the three pyramids. He stopped in the center, at the base of a huge mouse sculpture. It glowered over the surrounding land from its perch of what looked like half a globe, its thick, broken tail wrapping loosely around its base. A soldier was attached to one of its ears by a rope, and he swung across its face, coming to a halt by its eyes. The eyes glistened in the daylight like miniature suns, their beauty accentuated by triangular lines etched into the rock around them, fanning outward from their centers.

"What have you found, soldier?" asked Battersby.

The soldier seemed a bit surprised, but he stopped what he was doing and looked down.

"Diamonds!" he said, removing a crowbar from the bag on his back. "Two huge diamonds!"

The soldier dug the bar into the mouse's head and levered the first massive stone from its setting.

"That's quite a find," said Battersby. "Bring them to me once you have the second stone out!"

The soldier conspicuously hid a snarl by turning away, and Battersby walked off to the Great Pyramid, where he saw his right-hand man.

"Lord Battersby," said Smedley, saluting his commander. "We're about to enter the Great Pyramid."

"Good job," he replied. "I'm amazed by all these things you've discovered!"

Battersby was standing next to a pile of treasures,

ranging from silver pots and golden instruments to carvings and painted figurines of mice.

"Indeed, sir, we've found enough riches to bankroll an entire fleet of battleships!"

"This is marvelous news, Lieutenant, but I believe we have more than we can return with."

"Regarding that very problem, sir, I've been considering getting the men to fortify this area. A scouting party has just returned from the hills, and they found fresh water and a bountiful supply of wild fruit and food. We could create an outpost here, to guard and claim Norgammon for our own."

"That is a fine idea: we shall return with only the finest of the treasures, and focus on transporting the rare mice. They will stoke the fires of interest better for us, and increase the attention on Old Town until we can return with more."

"I'll set about preparing the mice for removal, then, sir."

"Excellent! And also try and contact the *Stonebreaker*—it must almost be finished in its task of charting the nearby seas and islands by now."

"Yes, sir!" said Smedley. "Once we've breached the Great Pyramid and have seen what is inside, then I shall make that my first concern."

Battersby picked up one of the bejeweled pots lying at his feet and let the sunlight catch on its golden rim. He was about to lift it to his eye when another soldier appeared at his side with a mousekeeper in tow.

"Lord Battersby!" said the soldier.

"We're not alone in the forest," said Miserley, butting in and resisting the need to play along with any formalities. Battersby had learned to trust her over the past year and had finally accepted her as a useful part of his team. She was now dressed in smarter clothes: those of a ranking Old Town Guard officer, rather than of a pirate's mouse-keeper, but her jacket was still buttoned tightly, and her long straight hair fell about her face freely.

"Our Sniffer Mice picked up the scent," she added, "and we've discovered the remains of a fire, still warm."

"Who could it be?" asked Battersby, slightly alarmed. "No one knows of this place but us. And we know Nor-gammon is uninhabited."

"Maybe someone has followed us?" said Miserley.

"No one could have followed us here; that's impossible!" said Battersby, angry at the mere thought.

"I don't want to speak out of turn," said Miserley confidently, "but you know full well who's capable of following you."

Lord Battersby looked aggrieved. It was clear that the very thought of Mousebeard having followed his ship was abhorrent to him.

"I cannot see how that blasted pirate would have heard about this!" he said.

"He's got friends all over the place," replied Miserley.

"One less than he did, now that we've seen to Lovelock's butler. But even so, this has been kept top secret."

Miserley brushed her hair out of her face and offered a suggestion.

"If they've followed us here, sir, then they'll want to know what we're up to. Why don't we set a few traps for them? Find out for ourselves who it is."

Battersby grew excited at the prospect of a manhunt, and he dragged a fingertip across his eyebrow.

"We have Sniffer Mice at our disposal, and Trapper Mice," said Miserley. "I also have vast stores of Popo

Explosives. If anyone treads on those, we'll know about it...."

"Popo Explosives?" asked Battersby.

"The droppings of the Popo Mouse," said Miserley. "They explode when they're trodden on—just a short, sharp shock and a loud bang. As soon as we hear anything, the Trapper Mice can be set free to see what they find."

"I like your style, Miserley," said Battersby. "Those Trapper Mice have sharp teeth, don't they?"

"It'll take a chunk out of you or me in one swift snap of its jaws."

Battersby started to laugh.

"I need to make use of these creatures much more than I do," he said, thinking of all the nasty uses he could find for the mice. "Talk to Lieutenant Smedley here about what you need, and I'll wait excitedly for the fruits of your labor!"

➤ ✳ ◀

Scratcher and Emiline walked slowly, their legs heavy with the feeling of being left out. They trudged behind

Fenwick and Algernon, who kept turning around to prod them along. Everything they said made them even more angry.

"Young mousekeeper...," grumbled Scratcher. "I'm no young mousekeeper!"

"No, nor me!" said Emiline, incensed.

"I'm at least as good as Indigo," said Scratcher ruefully.

Emiline gripped his arm and looked at him pointedly.

"Shall we go anyway?" she whispered.

"We can't," said Scratcher. "We'd be disobeying the captain!"

"This is different," she said.

"It is?"

"Yes..."

Scratcher felt his nerves tingling. His instinct told him it was absolutely the wrong thing to do, but he was with Emiline and it had been such a long time since they'd done anything like this together. He gave a little, awkward smile and stopped walking. He could prove to her he was as cool as Indigo.

"What have we got to lose?" he said.

"They'll be quite a way ahead of us now, but we're quick! We'd have to run!"

"I don't mind. It'd be better than going back to the ship."

Emiline watched Algernon and Fenwick walk farther into the distance and pass behind a line of trees.

"Ready?" she said, throwing a glance at Scratcher. Scratcher took a final look toward Algernon and then ran as fast as he could.

Moments later, Fenwick turned to find that the mouse-keepers had vanished. He ran to where he'd last seen them and hit a tree so hard he scraped the skin from his knuckles.

"Those stupid kids!" he said. "Where have they gone?"

Algernon joined him and chuckled.

"Mr. Fenwick," he said, "those young mousekeepers remind me of a young Mousebeard."

"They remind me of a big, fat pain in the butt!" Fenwick said, cursing. "Are we going to go get them?"

Algernon became more serious.

"I think they'll be all right," he said thoughtfully. "And

I think of more importance is that we inform Mouse-beard of Battersby's presence."

Fenwick clutched his throbbing hand and growled under his breath.

"Next time I see them I'm gonna give them what for!"

⇒ ❊ ⇐

Drewshank struggled through the undergrowth with Indigo. They'd been pursuing the small band of soldiers for almost an hour when they finally reached their destination. The forest ended abruptly, and they found themselves at the edge of a large stone-floored plaza, the outskirts of which were rough and broken due to age and marauding tree roots.

Indigo lay down behind a crop of thick tree trunks that were tangled together like a well-tarred ship's rope. He spied the open space before him and followed the two rows of carved towers that lined the sides as they led to the base of the golden pyramids.

The rest of the plaza was scattered with assorted tents in the form of a makeshift camp, and soldiers rushed back and forth, attending to one task or another. At the far side was a collection of hundreds of cages, some large and some small, but all filled with mice. Their unsettled and unhappy squeaking carried all the way into the forest. It was easy to see that most of the cages were far too small for their prisoners.

"They've caught so many rare mice," said Indigo. "How are they going to transport them all?"

"It's likely most of them won't make it," said Drew-shank. "Back in the old days, I took on a few missions like this. I wouldn't agree to it now, but we always caught twice as many mice as were needed—we knew a lot would perish on the journey home."

He passed Indigo his telescope.

"Take a closer look at the pyramids," he said. "Look what they're up to...."

The golden stepped pyramids were in a ruinous state, but they remained magnificent structures, with the largest rising to a few hundred meters tall. A decorated staircase was situated on its front face, and as it neared the pinnacle of the pyramid, it leveled into a small platform at the entrance to a chamber. This platform was the focus of much attention, and soldiers kept disappearing into it carrying barrels and other equipment.

The two smaller pyramids were much simpler affairs, although they too had chambers on top. Their steps were covered with strange objects and artifacts that had clearly come from within, and soldiers could once again be seen marching up and down them, with many carrying armfuls of goods.

"They're cleaning them out!" Indigo exclaimed.

"Have you seen the sculptures?" asked Drewshank.

Indigo peered closer at the base of the pyramids and saw sculptures of the purest gold and rarest turquoise glimmering in the bright sunlight.

"They must be priceless," he said.

"It's like the whole of the Mousing Museum at the Old Rodents' Academy has been brought out into the street!" added Drewshank.

Suddenly the soldiers rushed out of the chamber at the top of the Great Pyramid and hurried down a few of its steps before stopping. Along with an explosion, a big puff of smoke billowed out of its doorway.

"They've just blown something up!" he said, and as Drewshank's hand stretched out to his side, he passed the telescope back.

"Good grief!" said Drewshank.

Indigo slid onto his knees.

"I'm going to scout around the back of the camp and get an idea of how many troops there are," said Indigo.

"Good idea. If you're not back in ten minutes, I'll come and find you."

Indigo saluted and ran off through the trees.

⇒ ✳ ⇐

"Emiline! Look!" said Scratcher.

They'd arrived at the stone plaza and had slid behind two thick tree trunks for cover.

"The pyramids are amazing!" she replied.

"But look at all the soldiers! There are loads more than us. We're sunk!"

"Can you see Drewshank anywhere?" she said.

Both mousekeepers searched the treeline with their eyes but could see nothing.

"They must be somewhere," said Scratcher.

Emiline felt something brush past her leg, and she noticed a small line of mice rush past. Each mouse held on to the tail of the mouse in front with its mouth, and they wound through the undergrowth like a lumpy snake. As she moved her shoulder to look back at the plaza, she leaned on something small and hard, and a light explosion blasted beneath her. Her sleeve caught fire and she jumped away to try and smother it.

"Emiline!" cried Scratcher. He moved over to her, and his leg set off another explosion beneath him.

"What are they?!" said Scratcher, patting down his smoldering trouser leg.

"I don't know!" screamed Emiline, as another blew up underneath her.

The blasts and sudden movements had caught the attention of soldiers by the pyramids. One by one they picked up their rifles and pointed to the forest.

"Now we're in trouble!" she cried.

As the soldiers shouted to one another, another soldier came dashing into the plaza, followed by a girl. Three harnessed mice pulled him along, all champing at the bit to be released.

"They've got hunting mice!" yelled Emiline. "And that's…"

Emiline felt her whole body seize up as she saw the girl more clearly — she knew her from before.

"Miserley…," she said, snarling.

"We've got to run," said Scratcher. He took hold of Emiline and pulled her along into the forest, their feet setting off numerous other little blasts as they darted through the trees.

⇒ ❋ ⇐

"What on earth?" exclaimed Drewshank as he heard the cracks of explosions a few hundred meters from where he was hiding. As the soldiers charged to the treeline, he caught a glimpse of Emiline and Scratcher jumping into view and then running away.

"You can't be serious?" he said, withdrawing his sword. "I'm going to feed those blasted mousekeepers to some Nibbler Mice if the soldiers don't get to them first!"

He looked about for a sign of Indigo, but he was nowhere.

"Please, would someone finish me now...," he said, exasperated.

He looked for a final time at the pyramids and then ran back into the forest without another thought. Drewshank was able to run surprisingly fast when his mind was on the case: he jumped, twisted, and shimmied his way through the trees with the agility of someone half his size and age.

⇒ ✳ ⇐

After five minutes of running, Scratcher caught his breath and held on to the bark of a tree trunk to steady his weary legs.

"I can't keep running," he said, feeling as though he was choking.

Emiline was faring better, but she was struggling too.

"I can't believe Miserley is here," she said.

"Those hunting mice will be on to us in no time," said Scratcher. "We should have listened to Drewshank!"

"What is it with you?" snapped Emiline. "We made the decision and we can't change that now. Let's keep on — try and get to that ruin."

"All right," he said.

Emiline leapt over a fallen tree, hit the floor at speed, and then screamed out before being twisted and thrown upside down into the air on the end of a rugged chain. Her foot was caught in a metal mousetrap, and it was growing tighter and tighter at her ankle as she swung from the branch overhead.

"Emiline!" cried Scratcher.

He reached up and took hold of her hand.

"It hurts," she said, tears welling in her eyes.

Scratcher pulled at the chain and the trap, but everything was secure and unbreakable.

"I can't budge it," he said.

They heard the sound of whistles and twigs snapping nearby and knew their time was running out.

"Go!" she cried, with the trap tearing into her leg. "Go!"

"I'm not leaving you!" said Scratcher. "I'm not!"

"If you don't go, I'll hit you! Go on!"

Scratcher looked at her with desperation.

"I'll be back for you," he said. "I promise I'll be back."

He ran away as fast as he could, his emotions driving him on despite his lack of strength. Emiline started to feel dizzy, her head spinning from being held upside down for so long. She tried wriggling, and bending up to hold her leg, but the weight and the pain were becoming unbearable. The soldiers' footsteps were getting closer, as were the snarls and grunts of the Trapper Mice.

Suddenly they appeared.

"You don't look much like a mouse," said Miserley, smiling grimly beneath her flowing black hair as she appeared through the trees. She let a Trapper Mouse bound up to Emiline and growl at her head. Emiline could smell its foul breath, and she saw its fangs and foaming, rabid mouth were but a short distance from her nose.

"So you followed us all the way here, Blonde," she said. Her mouse, Weazle, scrambled onto her shoulder, its greasy fur and tatty ears reminding Emiline of how there was one mouse she hated more than anything.

"But where are your friends now, then? Are you here all by yourself? Surely not…"

"Shut up," snapped Emiline, finding few other words within her.

"And where's that useless Grey Mouse of yours? I know Weazle wants another bite of him.…"

Miserley walked around Emiline, gently pushing her so that she swayed from left to right.

"Captain!" she shouted. "We've got a prisoner!"

Emiline saw two soldiers walk into view, each holding a snarling mouse on the end of a lead.

"Take her back to camp and stick her in a cage with one of the Black-eyed Mice — the larger the species, the better," said Miserley. "That'll keep her occupied. And you'd better tell Battersby — if she's here, we can be sure there'll be others nearby."

Miserley took a final opportunity to push Emiline and inflict a little bit of pain as the trap tightened even further.

"Release the Trapper Mice," said Miserley to the soldiers. "We've got a hunt on...."

⇒ ❋ ⇐

"Captain Mousebeard!" shouted Fenwick. He stood beside the *Silver Shark* with sea spray washing over him as it flew off the rocks.

"Jonathan!" called Algernon, catching up with Fenwick. "We need to get defensive!"

After a few seconds, the gangplanks crashed down onto the causeway, and the pair walked onto the deck. Mousebeard's concern was clearly evident.

"The Guard is already here," said Fenwick.

"Battersby and all," said Algernon. "They beat us to it."

Mousebeard growled and teased his beard between his fingers.

"Where are the others?" he said.

"Drewshank and Indigo went to see what the Guard was up to. And best not to mention the mousekeepers...."

"Why? What have they done?" asked the pirate.

"They didn't follow orders," said Algernon, trying to suppress a smile. "Bring back any memories, Jonathan?"

"Maybe a few," he replied, laughing.

Fenwick struggled to see the funny side.

"But it's amazing in there," said Algernon excitedly. "The mice! Oh, the mice we saw."

"You must describe it all to me," Mousebeard replied. "And any clues regarding the curse?"

"We didn't see enough, Jonathan. I'm sorry..."

Algernon walked straight over to his little machine and

switched it on. The now accepted buzz-and-hum routine soon died down, and he watched the screen for any sign of movement.

"But if the Guard is here, where are the ships?" said Mousebeard. "I've seen nothing out here!"

"That's exactly what I'm trying to find out," said Algernon. "Ahh, I might have something here...."

Mousebeard knelt down next to his friend as Algernon pointed to the screen.

"That large yellow dot moving steadily around the island—that could be them!"

"Just the one ship?" said Mousebeard.

"If Lovelock wanted this kept secret, he may have felt that only Battersby could be trusted—it might be his big warship. It wouldn't surprise me in the least if it was!"

"Then we could take them in a straight fight," said Mousebeard. "If luck is on our side! What are we waiting for; let's set sail now!"

"I don't think that would be wise," countered Algernon. "A surprise attack might work, but I feel we'd be better off making use of our unique position."

"We could take some cannons from the *Shark* and arm

the ruins," said Fenwick. "Cover us on both sides, and make this outcrop our own."

"That way, however they come at us, they'll have to face a broadside," added Algernon. "And we can also block their path to Battersby—they would never leave without him. The walls of the castle—although there's not much left of them—are still thick and sturdy...."

"Aye, sir. It'd be a good defense," said Fenwick.

"By the mouse in the moon," said Mousebeard, "that's what we shall do. Get as many men as you can to help you. Take all the portside cannons and enough gunpowder and Powder Mice to see you through a fight. Send some men up to the gate too—if it's the only exit, it's the perfect place for an ambush."

"That's the spirit," said Algernon. "Like they set a trap for you at Giant Island, we shall have them at Norgammon!"

# The Halfung Hunting Mouse

A PROUD MOUSE, BRED FOR AGILITY AND POWER, THE HALFUNG HAS BEEN used in royal hunts for centuries. A native of Midena, it has become the most sought-after mouse amongst the landed gentry. Most usually kept in pairs, this mouse has an amazing sense of smell and is particularly noted for its obedience. Often seen in court paintings, sitting either side of the kings and queens of Midena, the Halfung Hunting Mouse is truly of blue-blooded descent.

### MOUSING NOTES

*This mouse requires much attention, in both grooming and play. Not an easy mouse to care for, it needs a diet rich in red meat—and a lot of it—so it can prove to be an expensive undertaking. However, what you put into this mouse will be rewarded in spades: it is a truly loyal creature.*

# The Great Pyramid

E MILINE WAS DRAGGED ALONG THE STONE PLAZA AND discarded at the base of a large cage. It was as tall as her and twice as long, and inside lay a mouse that almost filled it. A short chain was secured around its neck, stopping it from moving too far, but its weighty paws pushed hard against the iron bars, and its claws hooked out, scraping into the metal.

A soldier moved forward and unlocked the cage door, which he then lifted up, and with a firm shove forced Emiline inside. The mouse twisted to face her and hissed loudly, flattening its ears and lashing its tail about uncontrollably.

"There," he said laughing, "you've got a nice new friend to play with."

The soldier locked the cage and walked off at a pace. Emiline had barely enough room to sit down, and the mouse's tail continued to lash out at her. Each time it whipped her she clenched her teeth to suppress the pain. Seeing that she was now alone, she lifted the lid of her mousebox and was immediately berated by Portly, who squeaked and tried to rush up her arm. The mouse beside her burst back into life, opened its eyes, and started snapping its jaws, and Emiline quickly forced Portly back inside.

"I'm sorry," she whispered, as Portly squeaked inconsolably. "I'm sorry! It's for your own good!"

"There she is, sir!" shouted a soldier, and Emiline heard the scuffing of marching boots. She looked around to see Lord Battersby, who walked closer and laughed at her.

"You chose the wrong side, girl," he said, raising his sheathed sword and prodding the mouse that lay beside her. It squeaked and snarled and kicked out with its back claws, which cut across Emiline's leg like a series of razor blades. She screwed up her nose and bit her lip as she saw thin lines of blood appear on her leg.

"I did what was right," she said defiantly.

"Ha! What would a girl like you know about right and wrong?" he said.

Emiline looked into his eyes and caught hold of them. She wasn't going to be belittled by him.

"Your greed makes me sick," she said. "What are you going to do with all these mice? Do you know how important they are?"

"We know very well how important they are...."

Battersby's face became stern and he turned away.

"But you're just scum like every other pirate," he said, and he swung around, hitting his sword against the side of Emiline's cage. She jumped backward, shielding her face, and landed on the side of the mouse. It squealed horrendously and whipped its tail against Emiline's arm, making her cry out loud.

Battersby laughed again.

"So who *are* you here with?" he asked firmly.

"I came by myself...."

"Oh now, we all know that's not true. Was it Drew-shank? Did he follow me?"

Emiline kept her mouth shut.

"Or was it Mousebeard himself?"

Emiline still didn't say a word, and Lord Battersby's temper was about to boil over.

"You know you're only making this worse...."

He slammed his sword once more into the cage, and the mouse kicked, hitting Emiline in the stomach. She cried out and saw that its claws had sliced through her jacket, almost reaching her skin.

"Unless you want me to undo the chain around the mouse's neck so that it can feast on you," said Battersby, his voice determined, "I think you'd best tell me how you got here."

Emiline's thoughts descended on the *Silver Shark* and her friends. She pictured Mousebeard and remembered his rage.

"You realize Mousebeard will kill you," she said. "There's no way he'll let you get away with this."

"Ah...so it *is* Mousebeard," he said. He unsheathed his sword and pointed it through the cage at Emiline. "You realize that pirates, and anyone who disagrees with the might of Old Town, only ever end up dead."

"Not Mousebeard — he's far too clever for you!"

"Ah, I see," said Battersby, pushing the point of his sword gently under Emiline's chin. "As clever as that butler, eh? He didn't last long when a knife was run through him."

Emiline choked.

"It's amazing just how clever you all *really* are," he said evilly. "And yes, even the Old Town Guard has the ability to send long-distance Messenger Mice."

Battersby withdrew his sword from the cage and walked off.

"I'm going to leave you to stew a while," he said. "Think about what you've done...."

"You won't get away with this!" shouted Emiline angrily.

"Of course I will," he said, scowling.

⇒ ✳ ⇐

Scratcher threw himself into the ruin where they'd spent the night and collapsed against the tree that filled its inside. He didn't feel as though he had anything left to give.

"Thought you'd do a bit of spying on your own, eh?" said Drewshank, taking the boy by surprise. His face wore a stern and terrifying look, and Scratcher had never been so scared of him. "But where's Emiline?"

"They've got her," he said, struggling to speak. "She was caught in a metal trap...."

Drewshank shook his head.

"Do you see what you've done?"

Scratcher was so upset with himself that he wanted to cry. But that would achieve nothing other than making him look even more stupid and useless.

"Where's Indigo?" he asked.

Drewshank's expression didn't alter.

"I had to make the decision between helping you or waiting for him," he said. "I hope I made the right choice...."

Scratcher looked thoroughly depressed.

"But the Guard has been here already," said Drewshank, his tone lightening. "They would have known we were around anyway."

"I promise I'll make up for it," said Scratcher. "I really will."

"Impulse actions are strange things," he replied. "But it's often the case that they end up messy."

"Do you think Emiline's all right?" said Scratcher.

"I'm sure she is."

"But that Miserley..."

"Miserley?" said Drewshank. "Is she here?"

"She was with the soldiers."

Drewshank stopped talking at the sound of twigs snapping. The hunting mice were almost upon them—he could hear their snorting nearby.

"Do we run," said Scratcher fearfully, "or..."

Before he could finish his sentence, a bullet hit the wall next to him. He dropped to the ground and covered his head as another bullet left a pockmark in the wall.

"What the...," spat Drewshank, who also toppled to the ground. He took out his sword and held it tightly. "Looks like we might have a fight on our hands...."

Scratcher withdrew his dagger and noticed his hand was shaking. They both pressed themselves against the walls and tried to see where the soldiers were. There was no sign of them, but the Trapper Mice were closing in fast, judging by their growls.

"What do we do?" pleaded Scratcher, desperate for a way out of their situation.

"Have you ever been attacked by a mouse before?" asked Drewshank.

"Only little ones..."

"If they jump at you — and in this regard, I'm talking solely about the ones with big claws and teeth — punch them on the nose."

"On the nose?"

"Yes, or kick them."

"What's that going to do?" asked Scratcher.

"Not sure," said Drewshank, his eyes growing wide, "but I'm about to find out!"

A frenzied Trapper Mouse leapt into the ruin and landed straight on top of Drewshank. Its snarling jaws clamped onto his right arm, and he yelled as its teeth dug deeper. Scratcher jumped over and hit it hard on the nose before attacking it with his dagger. The animal didn't release its grip, and even when Scratcher stabbed it again, it continued to bite hard.

Suddenly a second Trapper Mouse jumped into the confined space of the ruin and ran for Scratcher. Just as he was about to attack it, one of the Old Town Guard appeared with his rifle aimed squarely at the boy.

"Don't move," he shouted.

Scratcher froze, as did the second mouse, which skidded to a halt, snarled, and paced back and forth around its prisoner.

"We've got two more of them," said the soldier, as Miserley walked up to the ruin's entrance with the third Trapper Mouse leashed to her side. The mouse biting into Drewshank's arm was losing a lot of blood and, quite noticeably, so was Drewshank. Miserley harnessed both of the mice and pulled them to heel, but the injured mouse faltered and slumped to the ground almost immediately. Within a few seconds its breathing had stopped.

Miserley looked tense and angry.

"Devlin Drewshank," she said, as he lay clutching his arm. "What a terrible surprise — just like a wart that you can't get rid of."

"Whatever made you so delightful?" he replied through gritted teeth.

"Your arm hurt?" she asked.

"Maybe you should learn to control your mice in the future."

"Oooh, you do scare me. And you, mousekeeper…"

She walked up to Scratcher and raised one of her daggers to his face.

"You'll soon be in much the same way. Tie them up!"

Two more soldiers arrived and tied the prisoners' wrists together. They took their weapons and lifted Drewshank to his feet. He was in a lot of pain and wished he could keep squeezing the bite on his arm to stem the flow of blood; it was bleeding profusely to the point that blood was running down to his fingertips and dripping in thick globules to the ground.

Miserley looked at her prisoners while stroking the dead Trapper Mouse.

"You two will pay for this," she said grimly.

⇒ ✳ ⇐

"So this is the marvelous Great Pyramid," said Lord Battersby.

He walked up the final few steps and entered the stone chamber. Lamps were dotted around, lighting up magnificent carved murals of giant mice with humans riding their backs in carriages. Battersby faced the doorway where his soldiers had blown a hole, and saw a tunnel lit by flaming torches descend into the bowels of the pyramid.

"Please go in, sir," said Smedley. "You won't believe your eyes."

Battersby marched down the sloping tunnel, followed by Lieutenant Smedley, and was immediately struck by the brightly illustrated walls and the airlessness. The farther he walked, the more glorious the pictures adorning the sides became, and more than once he had to stop and look in wonder at the depictions of ancient mice and people. The tunnel gradually grew steeper and narrower, and, at the point where it became an almost sheer drop, steps had been cut into the rock, making it possible to proceed. The staircase started to twist to the left and, as Battersby found himself stooping in order to carry on, he walked out into a high-vaulted tomb with three smaller anterooms joined to its sides.

Seated squarely in the middle was a stone coffin, its lid

encrusted with jade mice and inlaid gold details, and Battersby walked closer. He ran his hand along its surface and stroked the jade mice as if they were real.

"It's beautiful," he said.

"And the ceiling, sir?"

Battersby looked up and saw that the vaulted roof was shimmering like a starlit night.

"Diamonds, sir," said Smedley. "Worth a fortune alone."

"So this coffin and tomb are the prize of Norgammon," said Battersby. "Can we remove either of them?"

"The stone coffin's far too heavy, sir. But we may be able to remove the plaster on the ceiling that's host to the diamonds. We could recreate it in a museum setting, I'm sure...."

"Wonderful, and these other rooms?"

Battersby strode around the room and entered the anterooms. They were much plainer, but they also contained small stone coffins with jade decoration.

"We think it must be the tomb of a royal family, sir," said Smedley. "With the smaller coffins being for children, or something like that."

"That would make sense, especially with all these jewels sparkling above their heads...."

"And there is one more room through here..."

Smedley led Battersby into one of the anterooms, and at the farthest end there was a low passageway that led to another small chamber. Its thick stone door had been forcibly lifted by soldiers and was propped open by sturdy wooden poles.

"We think this room was maybe for another family member but ultimately never used," said Smedley. "It's next to empty, but for these pillars and a few decorated stone slabs."

Battersby looked through the doorway and nodded. It wasn't half as interesting as the main tomb, so he returned and looked back at the diamond sky.

"I still cannot believe that we've made such a discovery," said Battersby, standing with his hands behind his back as he looked upward. "This place is truly remarkable."

Suddenly, Locarno came running down the steps into the tomb.

"Lord Battersby!" he said breathlessly. "Two more

prisoners have been caught. One of them is Devlin Drewshank!"

"Are you sure?" said Battersby, his eyes glowing.

"Yes, sir. We are holding them outside!"

"Then I must come and see my old enemy with my own eyes!"

⇒ ❋ ⇐

"Oh, here he comes," said Drewshank aloud, as Battersby marched up to him with such pomposity that his head might have exploded.

Emiline was no longer trapped in a cage but was instead sitting alongside Drewshank and Scratcher. They all looked miserable as their arms were tied behind their backs, and they were about as happy as the caged mice held at the edge of the plaza. Miserley strolled behind the prisoners, kicking Emiline as she passed.

"What are we going to do with them?" she asked gleefully.

Battersby knelt down and smiled at Drewshank.

"Look at the mighty fugitive," he said. "I don't think I can be bothered returning them to Old Town. Mousebeard maybe — but not these three ruffians. I don't think anyone would miss them if they disappeared...."

"That sounds promising," said Miserley cruelly.

"Would you shut your mouth!" snapped Drewshank to Battersby. "You're making my ears ache!"

"You know," said Battersby, "you could have been something once. Beatrice was yours for the taking...she was beautiful, and maybe even loved you, but you just weren't good enough. And of course, I was a lord of the realm."

"Which is why she spends all her time with smelly mice these days," quipped Drewshank. "Far preferable to listening to your sanctimonious garbage."

"Ever the smooth fast-talker, Drewshank!"

"Better than the slow, witless wonder, Battersby!"

"Ha!" cheered Lord Battersby. "Even now you think you're clever. We know perfectly well where your ship is, and we're just waiting for the right opportunity to attack."

"Don't lie," said Drewshank.

"Lies? Oh you'd know full well if I was lying. You have no way of escaping this island now."

Drewshank felt his arm stinging below his shirt. The

mouse bite was hurting badly, and he did all he could to push the pain from his mind.

"And the problem of what to do with you three," said Battersby. "Well, I think I might have just the perfect solution."

Battersby turned away and caught the attention of Smedley, who was discussing the matter of the Great Pyramid with Locarno.

"Lieutenant," he called. "That tomb with nothing in it, would you mind me giving it a purpose?"

Smedley walked closer and looked at the prisoners. Smedley wasn't a bad man and didn't particularly agree with Lord Battersby's general views of the world, but he also wasn't a man strong enough to stand up to him.

"How do you mean, sir?" he said.

"I was thinking that I'd quite like to be rid of these three once and for all. How would you feel if we trapped them in that tomb—made it their final resting place?"

Emiline felt suddenly cold. Her fingers started to shake behind her back.

"It took ten men and a complicated winch to open that door," said Smedley. "It's as good a prison as any!"

"That sounds like a done deal to me, then! Take them

into the pyramid and remove anything that might be of use to them. Then, when you're satisfied, close the door and seal them inside forever."

Scratcher's heart was beating loudly, and he shifted sideways as he began to feel trapped.

"You are a worm," said Drewshank flatly. "You may remove us from your list of enemies, but there are plenty who will take our place. You won't leave this island alive."

"Oh, won't I?" said Battersby. "It's a shame you'll never know! Take them away."

Miserley dragged Emiline up onto her feet, and once she was standing, Drewshank and Scratcher were hurried to theirs.

"This way," said Smedley. He pushed them up the staircase into the pyramid and guided them through the tunnel. Miserley followed them, and when they finally reached the large tomb with the diamond-studded roof, they were allowed a moment to look around.

"It's beautiful, isn't it?" said Smedley, as much in awe of it as his prisoners, who were seeing it for the first time. "I'm sorry to have to do this to you, but orders are orders, aren't they."

Drewshank quietly wandered around, trying to find something that might sever his bonds, but he found nothing sharp enough.

"You're all such idiots," he said, trying to prolong their stay of execution.

"I'm sure it might look like that from your position," said Smedley, "but all that we do is for the good of Old Town, and ultimately Midena. Lord Battersby knows best."

"Lord Battersby knows nothing," said Emiline.

"That's enough, Blonde," said Miserley. "Where are we dumping them?"

"Through that room," said Smedley.

He led Drewshank into the anteroom and pointed to the smaller tomb that rested at the end of the passageway.

"In you go," he said, and pulled his sword out in order to look more forceful.

Drewshank walked in and saw the emptiness: it wasn't even a beautiful tomb, merely functional and boring.

Miserley pushed Scratcher and made him trip slightly out of surprise. He plodded reluctantly past Smedley, and

Emiline walked close behind. Once they were all in the little tomb, Smedley walked to the doorway.

"Now I know Lord Battersby wouldn't approve, but it seems only fair that I cut the ropes around your wrists. If you come here one by one, and then return to the back of the tomb, I shall be happy to do this for you."

"Are you crazy?" snapped Miserley.

"Absolutely not," he replied. "I'm just not a thug. You can do it if you like, and if there's any sign of trouble I shall show them the power of my sword."

Miserley looked unconvinced.

"Power of your sword? Are you mad? I'll cut just one of their ropes," she said, "and then they can untie themselves once we've shut them in."

"That sounds fair," he replied. "Boy! Come here."

Scratcher walked forward and turned around to show them his back. Miserley slid her blade between his hands and sliced upward. She then kicked his back and he flew back into the tomb.

"That's that then," she said, and she urged Smedley to finish the job. He gave an awkward smile to Drewshank and kicked away the wooden blocks that were holding back the stone door.

For a moment, the door teetered on its edge and then slammed into place with a heavy, booming thud. The prisoners were left in total darkness. The air was heavy and dry, and their situation looked completely hopeless.

⇒ ✳ ⇐

Lord Battersby readied a battalion of his soldiers in the plaza and watched them prepare for battle. They stood with rifles at their shoulders, awaiting further orders.

"Locarno," he said, "I've had enough of these insolent fugitives trying to get the better of us. I've been sent word that the *Silver Shark* is resting by the castle ruins outside the gate. It is ours for the taking, as is Mousebeard, and the *Stonebreaker* is ready for action."

"It sounds like we could attack them from sea and land, sir!" said Locarno.

"Exactly! If we force a march to the gateway, then storm through with full force as the *Stonebreaker* attacks…"

"They wouldn't know what hit them, sir!"

"What a wonderful thing that would be. And take those Trapper Mice—I like them and the damage they do."

Locarno stamped to attention in agreement.

As Smedley and Miserley walked out of the Great Pyramid, Battersby smiled in realization that the dirty deed had been done.

"Today just gets better and better!" he declared. "Get together thirty men, and let's march to war! I fancy showing Mousebeard the real might of the Old Town Guard!"

# The Popo Mouse

THIS UNASSUMING CREATURE LIVES IN THE FORESTS OF MILDUNG, AN AREA renowned for its wild chili peppers. After thousands of years living in this habitat, the Popo Mouse has grown such a tolerance for these spicy plants that it now eats nothing else—and with serious consequences. Its droppings are so volatile that they explode when squashed or trodden on.

If dried and stored safely, Popo droppings can be utilized in all manner of ways. The power of these explosive pellets is not life-threatening, but they will create a loud bang underfoot—certainly enough to provide an early warning defense system around your home.

MOUSING NOTES:

This mouse is rarely kept in collections, although the Old Town Guard is known to keep a whole building full of them in order to collect their droppings for military use.

# Scratcher's Surprise

THE DARKNESS SOON FILLED THEM WITH HORROR. Scratcher felt the ground, his fingers playing through the grooves in the stone slabs. The cold floor did nothing to raise his spirits.

"Emiline?" he said. "Captain Drewshank?"

"We're truly trapped this time," said Drewshank. "You see where your adventures have led us?"

"I'm sorry," said Emiline.

"I must admit that I expected better of you two," said Drewshank. "But staying angry is not going to achieve anything in here."

"Pass me your hands," said Scratcher, and he attempted to find them in the pitch black.

"There has to be a way out," said Emiline hopefully. "They always have ways out of these places."

"Do they now?" replied Drewshank. "And how many have you been stuck in before?"

"That's not helping," said Scratcher, as he untied his captain's arms.

"And there can't be much air in here either," added Drewshank, finally able to squeeze his wound tight to ease the pain.

"If only Indigo was here," said Emiline, feeling the rope loosen around her wrists. "He'd know what to do — or have some trick up his sleeve."

"Oh, will you just shut up about Indigo!" said Scratcher angrily. "Where is he now?"

"Look, if I have to stop moaning, you can ease up on that too!" said Drewshank. "I'm getting bored of your moods!"

Emiline realized that Scratcher really *was* jealous. Indigo had been right.

"Scratcher," she said warmly, trying to break the silent tension. "I'm sorry about things...you know. I've been trying to study hard and learn about mousehunting and…"

"It's all right," he replied quietly. "I understand. And Indigo *is* pretty cool.…"

"And in his favor," added Drewshank somewhat thoughtlessly, "at least Indigo might have had some of that explosive on him.…"

Suddenly, Scratcher thought of Indigo's boot. He hadn't said anything about it to Emiline or Drewshank before, but when Emiline had mentioned how wonderful Indigo was, back on the Mural Isles, he'd seen fit to try and copy him — and better him, even. And so, while with Algernon on the *Silver Shark*, he'd tried to recreate Indigo's shoes as a means of impressing everyone. With a kick of his heel, the base of his right boot flicked open.

"What was that noise?" asked Emiline. "What are you doing?"

Scratcher stretched forward, pulled out a match from his boot, and struck it on the floor. The room flickered into life, and he saw the look of amazement on his friends' faces.

"Where did you get that from?" said Emiline.

Scratcher lifted his foot and she noticed what he'd done to his heel.

"You've copied Indigo!" said Drewshank.

"I thought it was a good idea, that's all," he replied.

"What else do you have in there?" she asked.

The light from the match died, and the room fell into darkness again.

"Sorry, hang on...," he said.

Scratcher kicked his left foot, and the heel flicked around. This time he pulled out a miniature tin that resembled a matchbox, drew out a tiny piece of wick from a hole at its end, and lit it. This time the room was fully revealed in a warm orange glow.

"I can't believe you've done that," said Emiline.

"I've had a go at some of that explosive you said he'd had too...."

"Scratcher, my boy, I forgive you for being an idiot and getting us trapped in here!" said Drewshank. "How much do you have?"

"Not much," he said, "but then I don't know how powerful it is...."

"You've been running around with that stuff in your shoe, and you don't know how powerful it is!" exclaimed Emiline.

If the tomb had been glowing any color other than orange, Scratcher was sure they'd have seen that his face was bright pink.

"I haven't tried it yet," he said quietly.

"What are we waiting for?" said Drewshank. "Let's give it a go!"

Scratcher pulled out the first of two doctored lumps of Light Mousing Explosive from his exposed heel.

"By the doorway?" he said questioningly.

Emiline walked up to him and gave him the broadest smile she could manage.

"You really are something," she said, placing her hand on his shoulder. "Have you got a fuse?"

Scratcher fell silent.

"Not to worry," said Drewshank; "you can't be expected to think of everything. When I was back in prison, my cellmate always used to talk to me about his escape plan. It included using some explosive, which he planned to get smuggled in, and also utilizing his shoelace as a fuse. Ever since then, I've never worn slip-ons, just in case I needed one. Now would seem the perfect chance to try out his grand scheme!"

Drewshank pulled the lace from his boot and passed it to Scratcher, who threaded it into the clump of explosive and squeezed it into the almost nonexistent line between the stone door and the floor.

"Ready?" he said.

Emiline and Drewshank hid behind a square pillar, and Scratcher lit the shoelace. Once it was burning steadily, he joined the others. The fuse burned slowly—very, very slowly—and twice Emiline poked her head around to see it gradually shortening.

"It would have taken weeks to escape from prison with that!" said Scratcher.

"You're telling me!" replied Drewshank, and finally a very quiet *phut* sounded from where the explosive had been placed.

Scratcher looked out and saw a small black circle of charcoal dust on the door.

"Hmph," he said, and marched around to where the explosion was supposed to have given them freedom.

"Ah…," said Drewshank, as he and Emiline walked closer.

"It was a nice try," added Emiline.

Scratcher felt terrible. His shoulders slumped and he let out a long sigh of dejection.

"Hey, it could have been worse," said Drewshank; "it might not have gone off at all."

"Can I have your other lace?" said Scratcher, frustrated. He was determined the second lump of Mousing Explosive was going to work.

Drewshank frowned and thought of life without shoelaces.

"Don't you both have some?" he said.

The two mousekeepers revealed the buckles on their boots. Reluctantly Drewshank pulled his second lace free.

"This had better be worth it!" he said.

Scratcher took the lace, returned to the blocked doorway, and lit the fuse. They all strolled back to the pillar, knowing it would take ages to go off, and waited. They waited and waited. And then, suddenly, the most almighty explosion you could ever hope to witness blew a hole right through the thick door. Loosened rocks flew toward the pillar, ricocheting off and smashing into walls; ceiling plaster dropped to the ground in great clumps; and a cloud of dust surged backward into the room, covering everyone in grey.

Drewshank coughed and wiped dirt from his eyes.

"I'd say that bit worked then," he said.

The three friends looked at each other and burst into fits of laughter.

"Nice dandruff you have there, Scratcher," said Emiline.

"You're looking a bit pale today," he replied, laughing out loud. "Maybe you need to sit down?"

"Ah…," said Drewshank sadly, his spirits as demolished as the door, "but we've managed to collapse the passage."

The door was indeed shattered and in pieces, but there was now a pile of boulders blocking their path. Drewshank waited for the dust to clear and then stood up, shaking dust from his hair. He was about to try moving some of the boulders when a thick crack running along one of the stone slabs on the floor caught his attention. He wedged his fingers into it and started to lift.

"Quick, quick," he called, the weight becoming too much for him far too quickly.

Scratcher and Emiline took hold of the slab and lifted it higher, and eventually, with a great burst of energy, they sent it hurtling over onto its back. As soon as the slab was removed, a thick beam of golden light came shooting upward into the room. Everyone fell silent.

"I think we've hit the jackpot!" whispered Drewshank. His voice was filled with disbelief.

"What's down there?" said Emiline, almost speechless.

Scratcher knelt down and peered into the hole. He saw another tomb, but it was like nothing else in the pyramid. Norgammon had already overwhelmed him with its many colorful treasures, but the tomb was a treasure in itself: from the small amount he could see, he knew there and then it was special, for its walls were made solely of pure gold.

"Sir!" shouted Fenwick, his eye pressed to a telescope. "There's a ship on the horizon. It's the *Stonebreaker* all right!"

The *Stonebreaker* was a mean-looking vessel. Its darkened iron-clad bow was reinforced for extra strength, and residing below the bowsprit was a winged hammer figurehead. The ship stood higher in the water than the *Silver Shark*, and its three rigged masts cast a fuller, more imposing shadow against the light sky. Its cannon hatches were open, and its soldiers were at battle stations, ready for attack.

Algernon climbed on top of his submarine to look over the side of the *Silver Shark*. The ship was heading straight toward them, following the line of the massive wall and gaining speed all the while.

"It's at full sail," he said excitedly. "They're coming for us!"

"All hands to the cannons!" shouted Mousebeard. "Fenwick, get on land and ready the men."

"Aye, sir!"

"Algernon, what are you going to do?"

"I'm going to fight with you, of course!"

The pirate laughed and stretched up to shake his friend's hand.

"It's been too long since I stood at your side, Jonathan. Time to do my bit on the front line, as it were!"

"Indeed," bellowed Mousebeard.

"They're turning!" shouted Fenwick.

The *Stonebreaker* altered course to face the open sea, and although its starboard side was now fully exposed, it maintained its distance from them.

"What are they playing at?" said Algernon. "They're staying resolutely out of firing range....Where's the fun in that?!"

Suddenly, a blast rocked the *Silver Shark*, knocking it backward before it could right itself. Mousebeard rushed to the side, clambered up a set of steps, and leaned over. He could see pieces of wood rising to the water's surface. A volley of shouting surged through the ship from the gun deck.

"We're hit!" shouted a sailor.

"Hit?" screamed Mousebeard. "We're hit? By what?"

"There's water breaking into the hold, sir!" called the sailor. "We're patching it up, but it's a big wound!"

"Do your best, man!" ordered Mousebeard, and the sailor disappeared below deck once more.

Algernon spied the surface of the sea. His eyes trailed every peak of every wave, staring with such scrutiny as would have made anyone else's eyes hurt—but then he saw what he was looking for. A line of bubbles breached the sea: they were only faint, but his worst fears were realized. He jumped down onto the deck and started unbinding the ropes and chains that held his submarine in place.

"Change of plan! We've got to get me into the water," he yelled. "Jonathan, they've got submarines out there...."

"Submarines!" barked Mousebeard. "Since when?"

"They must have found my designs in my workshop," he grumbled. "Come on, help me—we don't have much time."

"But did they shoot at us from underwater?"

"Either that or they planted some sort of explosive on our hull...."

Mousebeard mustered two other sailors to help, and they soon released the submarine from its shackles. With sheer brute force they slid it along the deck until it was touching the side of the ship.

"We don't have time to lower it properly," said Algernon. "I'm going to get in; you open the gangplanks and push me off. It's a bit of a risk, but what isn't these days!"

Before Mousebeard could voice his reservations, another explosion tore into the hull of the *Silver Shark*. The deck tilted forward ominously and the sound of gushing water became all too clear.

"The low-down dirty...," growled Mousebeard, steadying himself.

"Come on!" snapped Algernon. He clambered up the ladder on the side of his submarine, lifted the hatch, and threw himself in.

"Just try and keep her afloat," he said, his head appearing through the submarine's hatch. "I'll go and see what I can do. You ready to push?"

Algernon sealed the door above his head, and Mousebeard saw his face appear behind the window at the front. The pirate banged the submarine's hull with his hand, unlocked the armored panels at the side of his ship, and ran to the back of the craft.

"Right then, men. On three.... One, two..."

With a hefty shove, the small submarine skidded along the deck and reached the edge. With one shove, it tumbled front-first into the water and, within a few seconds, was bobbing on the surface. The engine popped as Algernon ignited the controls, and with a splutter of a growl it disappeared into the sea.

Mousebeard ran down into the gun deck to find it almost deserted, but he knew exactly why. He charged along to the center of the deck and jumped down into the hold, where he was greeted with foaming, knee-deep water. All the gunners were frantically trying to board up the two gaping holes that threatened to sink the ship. Water was gushing in, blasting against the sailors and pounding into their efforts to hammer new planks and seal the breach. Panels of metal from the usually impenetrable hull twisted inward, and charred planks of wood were splintered and floating on the rising water level.

"Get to it, men!" shouted Mousebeard, resisting the urge to panic. "If you keep her afloat I promise to marry every one of you...."

"If we keep her afloat, sir," replied one of the sailors, "it'll be as much a miracle as one of the babies we'll have together...."

Mousebeard ran back upstairs and reached the top deck just in time to hear the sound of cannons firing from the castle ruins. The *Stonebreaker* was turning to take full advantage of the *Shark*'s predicament.

"Here they come!" shouted Fenwick, pacing around the ruined outcrop. "This time they mean business...."

→ ✳ ←

Algernon switched on his headlights, and he immediately became aware of his surroundings. The sea was shallow around the base of the wall, and although the murky water held more muck than air bubbles, he realized that Norgammon had once been much larger than the confines of the wall. He powered to the seafloor and could clearly see the remains of long-submerged stone structures. Seaweed-covered buildings and towers loomed dangerously out of the rocky bed, and Algernon could even make out the archways of a crumbling viaduct, now the home for many boggle-eyed Gill Mice who were clinging lifelessly to its pillars.

He pushed onward, swooping low through the powerful current. Treelike corals and giant clams stood out in the gloom, and the peculiar neon glow of sea life gave the underwater world a mystical life of its own as he navigated around ruined buildings. He slowed for a second and lowered his goggles over his eyes. He could see lights in the distance, moving haphazardly like Night-light Mice on a windy night. They were the very same submarines as he'd seen at Hamlyn, he was certain. He hovered for a minute and planned his course of action.

"Come on, old boy!" he said to himself. "It's now or never...."

He reduced the light from his headlights to a mere glow and let his submarine close in on the enemy. They were heading back toward the *Silver Shark*, and he knew that whatever else happened, they couldn't be allowed to strike again. Once he'd passed the submarines, Algernon twisted the controls and his craft turned a wide arc to fall in behind them. Their engines were stirring up the water, making it difficult for him to see farther than a few meters in front, but realizing he had no more time, he returned the headlights to full beam.

"This is *your* craft," he said to himself, "*your* craft... and *you* know what it's capable of!"

Taking no chances, he pushed the submarine to full

throttle and felt its power increase tenfold while its back kicked out slightly with the force. The engine didn't sound too pleased, but Algernon didn't care. He rocketed straight over the top of one of them, and just as the hull of the *Silver Shark* came into view in the distance, he let his craft push down. There was a loud crunch as the metal hulls collided, and Algernon screwed up his face with concern as he heard clang after clang chime below him. He pushed harder at the controls, and his vessel forced the enemy submarine downward; they descended gradually, both ships tightly and evenly matched, but Algernon's surprise attack had been enough. There was nothing the pilot of the craft below could do when his submarine plowed straight into a ruined stone wall.

Algernon sped sideways and looked across as a flash of light and cavalcade of bubbles indicated the submarine was no longer a problem. He veered away from the approaching *Silver Shark* and suddenly saw the other submarine in front. Its headlights were aimed directly at him, and he twisted sharply away. The two vessels narrowly missed collision, their sides scraping as they went their separate ways.

For the first time ever, Algernon dropped his hand to the floor and pulled up the safety belt that had found a permanent home beneath his chair. It buckled with a heavy click, securing him around the waist, and he returned his hands to his controls. He steered to the left, narrowly avoiding a lump of bedrock, and saw the lights of the enemy submarine in the rear viewfinder. It was gaining.

"Come on!" exclaimed Algernon. He tried to get more power out of his craft, but it couldn't manage it. He saw a mass of small bubbles appear from the submarine behind and had to take a second look: he realized there was a thick black missile approaching, its shape writ large in the glow of the lights. He turned the submarine sharply, and an explosion lit up a pile of rubble a short distance to his right.

"Missiles!" he cried. "How in the world have they managed that?"

Algernon's jaw dropped. He'd never seen fit to create underwater weapons, and he realized his shortsightedness. Even if they were copies of his submarine, the Guard had done a bit of work on them, he thought.

"Blast!" he cried, pulling hard on the controls, making

the submarine rise fast. It sped over the ruins, dipping and swerving through the arches of the viaduct, narrowly avoiding the torpedoes that were nearing with each shot. He could feel his engine grumbling at being overworked, and spurts of steam blasted into the cockpit. Algernon looked behind and could only see a line of bubbles rising to the surface of the water. And then his craft took a hit on its right side. It wasn't a missile: it was the submarine itself. He bent forward to get a better look, and the submarine returned for a second attack. It rammed him sideways, and he heard his right engine splutter and cut out. Algernon hurriedly flicked a switch on and off, but its power was gone, and he felt himself swerving uncontrollably from the thrust of the left engine.

He released the throttle to lessen the drift and felt his craft slow to a halt. The jolt had badly damaged his vehicle, and he cursed out loud, slamming the dashboard heavily. There was no way back without both engines, and he let the submarine sink to the floor. He unbuckled his belt and leapt up just as his craft was hit again. He stumbled to the left and heard the metal hull moan and groan. It was struggling under the pressure of the water and the dented side. He frantically threw his maps and any information that might be useful to the Old Town Guard into a waste chute on the floor. He sealed it shut, and with a press of a button it slipped away into the sea.

With little ceremony, he pulled the body section of his rotund underwater suit from the wall. It was quite a squeeze forcing his stomach through the narrow neck, but he was so used to it now that he knew what the power of breathing in could achieve. Once he was inside its shell, he tightened the buckles around his ankles and twisted a dial so that the hydraulic system responded to the movement of his legs. He walked forward to where the helmet was kept, stretched out, and lifted it down over his head before screwing it tightly into place. At the touch of another button, a small valve opened and air entered into the suit. Algernon clutched the levers that moved the robotic arms, walked to the submarine's hatch in a peculiarly lopsided fashion, and made all the right adjustments for an emergency escape.

Lights flashed up and down the cockpit as he flicked switches, warning him not to do what he was doing, but what choice did he have? With all of Algernon's actions, the submarine started to depressurize, and a thin trickle of water entered through the hatch. This grew into a steady stream, and finally, as the hatch flipped backward, an unstoppable flow of water flooded in. Algernon gripped the sides of the sub as it was buffeted back and forth by the rising water. He closed his eyes, waiting for it to ease, and then, when the water had taken over the sub completely, Algernon pulled himself free of the craft and floated into the deep sea.

With a firm tug of the other half of the stone slab, the path was clear for Emiline to slip down into the golden room. She dropped gracefully, and once her feet landed she stepped forward so that her friends could follow. The room was unbearably bright: six beams of light cut through the air, reflecting off every wall in a dizzying display of opulence. The beams originated from small holes built into the stonework that must have run all the way to the outside world, as the air was much fresher than that in the rest of the pyramid. Emiline was almost certain she could see the faint shapes of clouds being recreated on the floor where the lights hit.

The golden room was just a small box compared with what lay through a narrow doorway at its end, the entrance of which was an arch decorated with gold mice, whose tails all flowed upward and joined at its apex. Emiline walked through and stopped dead. She was in a long hallway, its walls glowing slightly green from the beautiful jade that covered them, and to her left and right were row upon row of mysterious mouse creatures, standing in deathly silence with their heads bowed. They looked the same size as humans, and they wore long dusty robes that touched the floor. Attached to the front of each robe was an armored chest plate, with a fine etching of a mouse carved into the metal.

On the creatures' shoulders were large mouseheads, built of a mixture of leather and metal. Some of them were terrifying, with horns jutting out from their noses, or thin spikes trailing down the back of their heads in between their ears. Their arms were also unusually elaborate, and instead of hands, they all ended in long metallic claws. They looked brutal, she thought, noticing their sharp serrated edges.

Emiline stepped closer and touched one of the creatures. When it didn't move, she poked it again and glided her hand across its features.

"Look at those!" exclaimed Scratcher, entering the room with a mixture of shock and excitement. "What are they?"

"They look pretty fearsome, don't they?" said Emiline.

"They look like warriors!" said Scratcher, walking closer and touching them for himself.

"Incredible!" said Drewshank, appearing behind them. He walked through the hall and stood eye to eye with one of the creatures. "There's a whole army of mouse warriors here...and Battersby has no idea."

Scratcher lifted one of the robes to find they were resting on clay mannequins that were as lifelike as any human.

"And look!" said Emiline, moving along. "There's yet another room at the end!"

She ran forward along the stone floor and came to a second archway, which was sealed with a dark wooden door; iron strips ran along it for strength and effect, and the tip of each bolt that joined them was in the shape of a mousehead. There was a handle on the door's left side — it was in the shape of a curled mousetail, and Emiline took hold of it. With a firm push, she twisted it downward and felt the door open.

# The Dum-Dum Mouse

THIS RARE, BLACK-FURRED MOUSE CAN ONLY BE FOUND ON DIM-DIM ISLAND, *a place where the sun barely lifts above the horizon because of its close proximity to the Southern Pole.*

*Living in a world of perpetual twilight can do strange things to a creature, and the Dum-Dum is quite extraordinary for its hollow, barrel-shaped chest. When it feels threatened, or when turning a corner on a narrow mouse track, the Dum-Dum rears up on its hind legs and thumps its enormous chest like a drum to let other creatures know it is there. This pounding noise not only gives the mouse its name, but also gives would-be predators the impression that it's much larger than it actually is.*

### MOUSING NOTES

*Its rarity makes it an exclusive mouse found only in the richest collectors' mouseries.*

# The Tomb of the Mouse King

WHEN INDIGO RETURNED TO FIND DREWSHANK GONE, he feared the worst. He knelt down on the forest floor and touched the ground gently, looking for any signs of a fight. There were none, but eventually he spotted a line of delicate branches that had been snapped in two, and he realized Drewshank had left in a hurry. He followed the tracks all the way to the ruins, running as fast as he could. He found the marks of a gunfight: the dead Trapper Mouse and a pool of blood that had left a darkened shadow on the mossy floor. Indigo leaned back against the tree for a moment to think things through.

Norgammon was a world very similar to his own: the pyramids, forests, and marvelous ancient ruins were all so similar to his homeland that he felt quite at ease in its company. He was so used to working alone that he could quite happily have stayed there and forgotten about the plight of Mousebeard, Drewshank, and his crew. But then he remembered Emiline, and the friend that she had become — he couldn't let her down.

Indigo untied his ponytail and let his hair fall to his shoulders. He unbuttoned his grey jacket to reveal his cotton undershirt and, once he felt ready, righted himself. He'd never planned to fall in with Mousebeard — in fact, it had been the exact opposite of his plans. Before he ever reached Hamlyn, he'd sworn to do his duty to his country and find out the truth, and here he was, finally fighting against the true enemy. All his preconceived notions and prejudices had fallen by the wayside, and he decided to return to the *Silver Shark* to continue the fight.

He ran through the forest, trying to remember the path they'd originally taken into Norgammon, but it was so difficult to be sure. He found a tree to climb and scrambled up as fast as possible to take a look out at the wall. Once he had a clear view, he soon realized where he was heading, as he could see the platform and the entrance to the island. Just as he was about to jump back down, something caught his attention on the flight of stairs that led up from the ground. There was a long line of people marching upward at quite a speed. It suddenly dawned on him that it was the Old Town Guard, and he realized he had no time to lose — they were launching an attack.

He dropped down and opened his mousebox so that his Sharpclaws could run onto his shoulders; they did so happily and gripped tightly with their back paws, letting their tails fall back to give them balance.

"Ready to fight?" he asked, seeing their shining front claws hang over his shoulders.

Emiline pushed at the door and it swung heavily and squealed loudly, probably due to the fact that it hadn't been opened in thousands of years. The scene that greeted her topped anything that had gone before.

The room was squarer and larger than the previous hallway. Carved murals adorned the walls, each one painted in colors that sang out like a rich tapestry. Pieces of gold were inlaid at points of interest, and they shimmered with the light that burst down through a single hole in the roof. Like a thick band of ribbon, the light poured down into the center of the largest coffin in all the pyramid. It stood at almost a meter high, and its convex lid glistened with the richest of jewels. Set proudly in the middle of the beam of light was a gold mouse, standing up on its hind legs, and if it weren't for the fact that Emiline had seen the other coffins and the other mouse statues on them, she'd have thought it was a *real* Golden Mouse.

Emiline walked around the room, studying the walls. One character seemed prominent in all of them: he was wearing an outfit much like those they'd found in the previous room, and upon his shoulders were small white mice, their eyes a bright blue. As she progressed from picture to picture, she realized she was reading a history of Norgammon: from a depiction of the pyramids being built, to a strange scene of high waves crashing against towns and buildings, and an even more vivid image of giants constructing the wall around the land.

When Drewshank walked in, he found Emiline in a near trance, so taken was she by the imagery.

"Giants built the wall," she said, enlightened. "It all makes sense! That's how it's so big."

"Giants?" said Drewshank.

He looked at the pictures and followed the history of Norgammon just as Emiline had done.

"And this tomb?" he said.

"I think this is *his* tomb...," she said, pointing to the main figure. "He was the one who built the pyramids. He must have been the king."

"Look at all these jewels!" said Drewshank, touching the surface of the coffin, feeling the cold hardness of the thousands of gemstones. "I could buy a new ship with all these...."

"And there are his mouse warriors!" she said, finding a carving at the end of the room depicting hundreds of the warriors standing at the base of a pyramid with the king at the top. They all had the same strange white mice on their shoulders.

"And a pure gold mouse!" said Drewshank, stroking it gently, his hand being lit fully in the light. "I bet that's worth more than any of Lady Pettifogger's monsters! With all these things we'd be rich!"

"You're starting to sound like Lord Battersby," said Emiline reproachfully.

Drewshank's head fell as he realized she was right.

"But what's this?" she added.

She was staring at an image of the Mouse King, his arm outstretched and holding a white mouse. Its body was glowing bright blue, the light bursting out of him like the rays of the sun. Numerous humans were scattered below him; all of them looked to be in pain: some were screaming, some had their heads in their hands, and others were lying dead.

"I don't like the look of that," said Drewshank. He passed his hand once more over the gold mouse and felt it slide forward.

"It moved?" he said, touching it again and finding that it shunted forward before toppling over fully.

Suddenly a series of knocks and clunks sounded from the stone coffin, and Emiline turned to look at Drewshank.

"What have you done?" she said.

"I did nothing!" he pleaded, clutching his head.

Emiline saw a series of holes open at the base of the coffin.

"Captain, what have you done?!"

Drewshank tried to replace the gold mouse, but it wouldn't stay upright. He felt that strange feeling that often washed over him before something bad happens.

"Okay," he said, "I'm going to keep calm." He shuffled back to the door and was soon joined by Emiline.

They watched the holes as though their lives depended on it. Just as they started to feel better about themselves, an old, hairless mouse crawled from one of them. Its eyes were dim, and its movements slow. A second, a third, and a fourth followed it, and eventually mice were streaming from all around. The first ten or so all looked the same, but as their number increased, their ages seemed to get younger, and with it the quality of their coats. Some of them even looked as though they had white fur.

"It's fine," said Drewshank; "they're just mice. We can rest easy."

Emiline realized what species they were almost right away.

"They're Methuselah Mice," she said.

"They are?"

"Some of them are just like the one we found on Stormcloud Island! So that woman did come here...."

The mice crawled onward, their opaque eyes focused on Emiline. There were at least thirty of them by now, and their number continued to grow. Their wrinkled, almost hairless skin twitched and shivered, and as they grew closer, they started to salivate and drip ooze from their mouths.

"Don't move!" whispered Drewshank. "They're right next to you...."

"I'm trying not to," she said, as the Methuselah Mice crept over her feet. The feel of their small bony paws was enough to put her on edge.

"Why are they here?" said Drewshank. "What on earth are these mice doing in here?"

Emiline bent down to pick one up, and a blue glow erupted from the mouse and started to spread around the room. As if it was part of a chain reaction, the glow seemed to pass from mouse to mouse, until they were all bathed in blue light.

"Right," said Drewshank. "That's not a good sign...."

"I don't think we wanted that to happen," said Emiline.

The blue light grew brighter until all the mice were fizzing like lightbulbs, and their eyes, no longer blank and dead, were as blue as the sky.

"It's heating up in here!" said Drewshank, a tingling, buzzing feeling growing in his cheeks, and sweat forming on his brow.

Emiline took a step back and narrowly avoided three of the mice that were staring straight at her.

"Oh no…," she said, deadly serious. "We've got to get out of here. We've got to run! I know what this is!"

"What?" said Drewshank. "What is it?"

Emiline turned to run but froze on the spot. Directly behind her, standing at the doorway, was one of the Mouse Warriors. It was alive, and terrifying. She swallowed heavily and her lips trembled. Strong shadows cut across its head, highlighting its features and making them seem even more intense. It raised its nose and seemed to be sniffing her. With a jittery movement, the creature's head twisted to the side, sending its thick ears and long whiplike cords swinging backward. The Mouse Warrior lifted its hand toward Drewshank and its four serrated claws glinted in the light.

"Oh blazes...," said Drewshank. His legs wouldn't move. "What more's going to come out of this blasted tomb!"

The Mouse Warrior stepped farther into the room, and the bright blue light dulled until it was a faint glow. The mice crawled away from Emiline and Drewshank and headed straight to it.

"Emememm!" it said.

"Did you hear that?" whispered Drewshank. "It spoke!"

With the Methuselah Mice arranged at its feet, and two sitting on each of its shoulders, the Mouse Warrior spoke again.

"Dressshhn...sme...Sssscrrrrrrshr!"

The Warrior lifted its claws and scratched its helmet.

"Is that you, Scratcher?" said Emiline.

"Ysss...corssse!"

"It's you!" cheered Drewshank, almost feeling he wanted to cry.

Emiline walked up to Scratcher, but the mice clustered around him started to glow brighter. As she retreated the glow dimmed once more.

"They think you're a real warrior—I think they're trying to protect you," she said.

"Yooo thnk?"

"I do! Try walking away!"

Scratcher made a few paces backward, the light robes flowing gracefully around his legs. The mice followed him as if they were loyal servants under the power of their leader.

"That's the ticket!" said Drewshank.

"The Methuselah Mice," said Emiline, "and that glow—it's just as Mousebeard described."

"Of course!" said Drewshank. "The Methuselah Mouse on Stormcloud Island was defending her."

"That's it!" said Emiline. "It was the mouse that cursed him and Isiah, not the woman—she was no witch!"

"But that was just one mouse," said Drewshank. "All these mice seem to be joining their powers...."

The immensity of the situation dawned on Emiline.

"Just imagine what harm they could do as one!" she said.

"We have to tell Mousebeard!"

"We have to get to him before Battersby and the *Stone-breaker* do! He could have the key to breaking his curse right within his beard!"

Drewshank gripped his chin.

"But we have no way out!" he said, as it dawned on him that they were still trapped.

Emiline walked to the coffin and looked through the small holes at its base. She sniffed the air and found that it was fresh.

"There's a tunnel down there! Those mice must have come from somewhere! Help me lift off the lid."

Forgetting the fact that Scratcher was covered in Methuselah Mice for the moment, Drewshank and Emiline pushed against the stone coffin.

"Did it move?" asked Drewshank, imagining things.

"Scratcher, come give us a hand!" said Emiline.

The Mouse Warrior walked forward, bringing his glowing friends with him. He stuck his claws into the gap between the lid and pushed upward. A powerful blue glow fizzed around his hands, and the stone lid moved across with ease.

"I've got to get myself one of those outfits!" said Drewshank.

Inside the coffin, resting across a metal grate, were the bones of a human. Whoever had been inside had long perished, but sections of the mouse armor remained, including a golden pendant of a spiraling mousetail.

"And look below the bones," said Emiline, pushing some aside to see through the grate.

The glow of the Methuselah Mice lit up a wide tunnel that sank low into the ground and then disappeared from sight.

"That's our way out!" she said, laughing aloud. "We've done it!"

≫ ✳ ≪

Algernon landed on the seabed and looked all around for signs of the second submarine. The murky water had grown murkier since their battle. The beams of light issuing forth from his eyes gave him a general idea of what was in front of him, and he aligned himself with where he thought the *Silver Shark* was situated.

"Do it!" he said, and before his nerve could give in, he

flicked a switch that sent blasts of air out of the back of his suit. He went soaring through the water, passing over ruins and piles of stone. Suddenly, the black mass of the *Silver Shark* and the rocky outcrop behind it zoomed into view. He cut the power to his air jets and tried to steady himself.

He'd been traveling at such a speed that his suit kept on sliding forward. His feet skidded into the sandy floor, and he teetered on one leg as the momentum took him closer to the hull of the ship. Once he'd stopped and his beating heart had slowed, he realized he was standing right below the damaged section of the ship. It had been patched up well and looked fairly watertight, although he could tell that it wouldn't survive a journey at sea.

"Where are you, then?" he said, turning around. "Show yourself!"

As he searched the water, squinting to try and see farther, he caught sight of an explosion coming from the distant seabed. A faint flash of light carried to him, and he guessed that it had been his submarine.

"No choice now, then," he said to himself. "Got to keep this ship afloat!"

When the second submarine returned to his line of sight as just a faint black blob in the distance, he realized that against those torpedoes, there was only one course of action. The submarine drew closer and closer, its headlights beaming brightly. Algernon pulled a lever, and the second robotic claw rotated to reveal the drill piece; he tugged another lever, and the other claw shot forward so that it was ready for use. He swallowed hard and twisted himself to the right so that he was in line with the submarine. The seconds passed, and then just as the submarine had reached shooting distance, he switched on his air jets and went flying diagonally upward, directly into its path.

Algernon switched on the drill, and with the jets pushing him at full speed into the bright headlights, he thrust it forward. The pilot became visible—his mouth wide open in disbelief. Algernon closed his eyes and with little thought for his own safety aimed straight for the glass windshield. With his drill whirling at top speed, he rammed it into the glass as his suit made contact. Sparks shot out like fireworks. The hit knocked Algernon hard, and his suit bounced like a rag doll over the submarine, spinning out of control. His head hit the side, the suit crumpled inward and squeezed into his leg, and the interior lights died out. He caught sight of the submarine careering into the seabed. The windshield had shattered. Algernon slammed hard at a small green button as darkness descended and clouded his thoughts.

# The Northern Musical Mouse

THE NORTHERN MUSICAL MOUSE WAS DISCOVERED ON THE ISLAND OF *Widdly Rock by Gregarious Garner, the famous Mousehunter. The mouse earned its name because of its unusual habit of knocking on pieces of dead wood to create a lively form of mouse "music." This act coincides with the mating season, and it's thought that a mouse will only deem a mate compatible if he or she is playing a similar tune.*

### MOUSING NOTES:

*These mice like to be kept in small groups and must never be kept alone. They require very little special treatment, other than allowing for their necessity to make noise when the mating season arrives (and they do like to make a lot of noise). As an added aside, their wavy grey fur with hints of bronze can look terrific if lit properly, so a good lighting setup can be beneficial.*

# The Battle for Norgammon

F ENWICK BOUNDED FROM ONE CANNON TO THE NEXT within the castle ruins, providing direction for his gunners. They were placed wherever there was a direct view out to sea, generally in spaces where the walls had long fallen: the ruins weren't a perfect defense, but they were better than nothing. A group of Powder Mice were busy at work too, seemingly relishing the new conditions. They hurried along, providing gunpowder without any fear. Fenwick could see onto the deck of the *Silver Shark*, and he caught the eye of Mousebeard.

"The *Stonebreaker*'s turning again!" he shouted.

Mousebeard heard his call. He bellowed new orders to his sailors.

"She's coming back around! Get them cannons ready!"

The *Stonebreaker* was a few hundred meters away, in full sail. Its cannons were aimed at the *Silver Shark*, and as it sailed past the outcrop into the ship's eye line she unleashed her first broadside. Clouds of smoke erupted from her side, and Mousebeard threw himself to the ground as cannonballs flew his way with abandon, hitting not only the ship's hull, but also the outcrop behind.

The pirate regained his composure and returned to his feet. He pulled a pistol from his belt and shouted with all his might.

"Take aim and FIRE!"

Instantly, the cannons roared from the *Silver Shark*, their load smashing into the *Stonebreaker*. Most of the shots hit their target, with two flying straight through the sails. Splinters of wood flew into the air, and a loud cheer rose up from the gun deck.

"Fire at will!" boomed Mousebeard. He ran to the helm to look out over the sea at the attacking vessel.

"Captain!" called a sailor from the castle ruins. "There's fighting at the gate!"

The pirate glanced at the farthest point of the winding path and watched puffs of smoke rise with the firing of rifles. He removed the telescope from his belt to get a better look. His men at the gate were running down the path in retreat, and he watched each one fall as six large mice sprang into view and leapt at them. The men desperately tried to break free of their claws, but there was no way of escape.

While the men struggled with the mice, a row of soldiers walked up to the sailors, raised their weapons, and shot at point-blank range. Mousebeard steeled himself as their bodies slumped to the floor before being kicked over into the sea.

"This is going to be the end of one of us, Battersby," he growled furiously. "Fenwick! We need to halt the soldiers' path!"

On hearing his words, Fenwick ran through the ruins, slid down the slope, and stopped at the side of the *Silver Shark*.

"We what?" he said.

Mousebeard stomped toward him.

"The Guard is approaching. We need to blow up a section of the path to stop them from reaching us."

Fenwick saw the line of soldiers advancing along the causeway in the distance.

"But Drewshank and the mousekeepers! How will they reach us?"

"Mr. Fenwick, do as I say."

"I can't," he replied. "I ain't leaving my friends stuck behind."

"We haven't got time for this, man. Without this ship, we're all lost!"

Fenwick frowned and clenched his fist. He wanted so desperately to disagree with the pirate, but he knew he was right.

A new round of cannon fire shot across the sea from the *Stonebreaker* and hit the starboard side of the *Silver Shark*, causing damage to the hull and gun deck. Cries of horror echoed through the ship and Mousebeard stumbled forward and cursed aloud.

"Blast you, Fenwick! Do as I say!" barked the pirate.

As his face paled, Fenwick knew what he had to do.

⇒ ✳ ⇐

Lord Battersby considered the *Silver Shark*'s position from the gate at the top of the path. A smile passed over his face as he watched the *Stonebreaker* unleash its arsenal.

"There's no way that the pirate will escape this," he said, waving more troops forward to continue the attack.

"They're in control of the ruins as well," said Locarno. "They have cannons and maybe a few muskets and pistols, sir."

"No worry," said Battersby. "They don't have the manpower to deal with an attack on two fronts. With the *Stonebreaker* forcing all their cannons to focus on her, we can take aim from the relative safety that distance will give us. Let the Trapper Mice run free to hunt them down."

"I'll lead them myself, sir!" said Locarno.

He stamped to attention, clutching the base of his rifle. Rufus Locarno was a determined and focused man, and he collected his troops and ordered them to follow him.

"If you provide us with backup, should we need it, sir," he said.

"Of course!" said Battersby, his pistol at the ready. "I shall keep right behind you."

⇒ ✳ ⇐

"The ship's coming back round to our side!" shouted Fenwick to the men within the ruins. "Don't wait to be told to fire!"

He held a small barrel in his arms, and he watched the Old Town Guard close in—they were now only about ten minutes' march away, and time was running out. He ordered a sailor to join him, and he breathed deeply before setting off again. He jumped from the outcrop and hit the path running. As the path started to rise, at a good distance from the *Silver Shark*, he kicked a few of its large cobblestones over into the sea and made a nest for the barrel.

"Keep an eye on them troops and mice," he said to the sailor. "If they get within shooting distance, fire!"

The sailor raised his weapon to his shoulder and trained it on the approaching group. He could see the hunting mice bounding toward them, following the curving path like a racetrack.

"The mice are getting closer, sir."

Fenwick drew out a short fuse.

"How close?" he said.

"Very..."

Fenwick was about to light the fuse as the sailor fired. He hit one of the mice, and it wailed and flew backward.

"Got it, sir," he said, reloading as fast as he could.

"Almost done...," said Fenwick. "Right, when I say 'now,' run!"

The sailor lifted the weapon once more and saw that the mice were just a hundred meters away. He fired again and hit another one.

"Four more to go!"

"Now!" shouted Fenwick.

The two of them sprinted back down the path and threw themselves onto the *Silver Shark* as the barrel of gunpowder exploded. Rocks flew into the air, raining dust and grit onto the deck beside Mousebeard. The pirate viewed the spot where the barrel had been and saw there was now a two-meter-wide break in the path, with nothing but the sea below.

"Perfect," he said triumphantly, "but it won't hold them forever."

Fenwick looked back at his handiwork and saw the

hunting mice launch themselves over the gap he'd made in the causeway.

"Those blasted mice!" he said.

Mousebeard pushed him to one side and held his pistol at full stretch before firing. He hit a mouse, and it fell into the path of two others. They all cascaded into the sea, their squeals piercing the air as they hit the jagged rocks below. The fourth one kept coming at them. Mousebeard threw down the pistol and pulled another from his belt. The mouse bounded ever closer, its back legs kicking the ground furiously, and before the pirate could take aim it jumped onto the ship. Mousebeard widened his stance and held the weapon aloft.

The mouse's claws scraped over the wooden deck as it veered past the pirate and leapt straight at Fenwick. He stood firm, with the full weight of the Trapper Mouse about to hit him in the chest. Mousebeard turned and aimed his weapon.

Fenwick held his breath: seeing the barrel of a gun pointing straight at his head was enough to give him a heart attack. But luckily, Mousebeard was on target. Without a moment wasted, he fired again. Fenwick went flying backward and landed heavily on the deck. The mouse lay dead on top of him.

Mousebeard pulled at the lifeless creature and threw it aside. Fenwick's face was covered in blood, but all he felt was relief that Mousebeard was such a good shot.

"It won't bother us again," said the pirate playfully.

⇒ ✳ ⇐

Indigo emerged into the light with his mice a short distance in front. What was left of the iron gates had been opened wide, and he crept around their rusted panels. The battalion of soldiers was about halfway between him and the ship, marching forward with intent. He could see the *Silver Shark* through a cloud of smoke, and ant-like sailors running to and fro amongst the ruins, their cannons blazing as the *Stonebreaker* coursed across the waves. The battle was fierce, and he realized it was time to act.

He gestured to his mice, and they scampered down the steep path, their claws raised. They were much faster than him, and he let them rush ahead while he went at his own pace. The path zigzagged closer to the action, and at a point where its level dipped, Indigo dropped to the floor and hid himself from view, only lifting his head every few moments to check on the direction of his mice. He'd decided to let them do the hard work for him.

"Draw blood for Illyria…," he said.

&#8680; &#10033; &#8678;

Locarno rested his rifle in his arms and surveyed the *Silver Shark*. He'd made good progress and was now standing at the break in the path with his troops behind him. The *Silver Shark* was but a few minutes' walk away, but he chose to wait. He'd seen the Trapper Mice suffer at the hands of the pirate, and he required Battersby's advice.

"Wait here, men," he said, ordering his soldiers to form a line and aim their weapons toward the *Silver Shark* and the ruins.

He returned to Battersby, who was standing a short distance up the causeway.

"They've blown a hole in the path, although it's not such a distance as to be impassable, merely a pain. What do you suggest we do, sir?"

Battersby seemed intrigued by the news.

"So they've cut themselves off from the mainland by their own actions? That's interesting...," he said.

The *Stonebreaker* fired its cannons once more, hitting the ruins full on. He heard the cries of Mousebeard's sailors as the outcrop shed a flurry of rocks into the sea.

"There's only so long they can maintain their position," he added. "Keep your men as they are. Block their passage and make sure they can't escape."

"Yes, sir!" said Locarno. He saluted and made his way back to his troops.

Battersby puffed out his chest and teased his mustache.

"I believe we have won this," he boasted.

"Sir!" said a soldier. "There are two mice running toward us!"

Battersby looked up the path and took a few steps forward.

"They look like a familiar species," he muttered.

The mice reached the first few soldiers standing unaware on the path, and they attacked. They launched into the air, swinging their paws back, and with swift cuts of their claws destroyed the soldiers' weapons and then went in for the kill. Trained assassins as they were, the mice dispatched two of the soldiers and jumped at another, but before they could reach him he'd leapt off the path in terror.

"Sharpclaws!" shouted the onlooking soldiers.

The mice attacked again, causing panic to spread along the lines. The causeway was too narrow for any such behavior, and Battersby called for calm. He readied his pistol.

"Clear the way!" he barked, storming forward to meet the mice. He was never afraid—particularly not of animals.

"Haven't you ever heard of shooting things?"

He spotted the first Sharpclaw and aimed right at its head. Without a second thought he'd pulled the trigger and killed it outright. Battersby stretched across to take a rifle from one of the soldiers and aimed it at the next. The Sharpclaw reared back as if to jump, raising its claws into the air, but he didn't take any notice. As it leapt at him, Battersby swung the weapon around in his hands and smashed the surprised mouse with the rifle butt. It went flying from the path and plunged into the sea.

Battersby laughed triumphantly.

"The mice are gone now. You can rest easy...."

Having seen what Battersby did to his mice, Indigo jumped up. He wore a deathly expression, and he ran at full speed toward Battersby with his sword high in the air.

"And just who is this?" said Battersby, pushing the rifle butt into his shoulder and targeting the boy.

Indigo gained ground, his feet pounding under him as he pushed hard. His black hair trailed behind him, lashing against his back with every step. Battersby waited for him to draw closer, and then, when Indigo was just ten meters away, he pulled the trigger.

After withstanding repeated assaults by the *Stonebreaker*, the outcrop and the ruins on top were suffering badly. Successive blasts had weakened the remaining walls, and most of the stonework was now lying in the sea. The cannons and gunners were now fully open to the *Stonebreaker*'s onslaught, and it wasn't just cannon fire: the ship was sailing ever closer and snipers were picking off sailors at every opportunity.

Mousebeard watched the situation grow ever worse. The *Silver Shark* had taken too many hits to its armor and the seams of the metal hull were breaking apart.

"Fenwick! Bring everyone back on board!" he ordered.

"About time! We're sitting ducks up here!" he replied.

The remaining sailors ran through a torrent of cannon fire before they jumped down onto the path and made it to the relative safety of the ship. Mousebeard hurried them all onto the deck.

"What about the ropes?" cried Fenwick, dragging a wounded sailor up onto the deck. "I won't be able to cut them all...."

"No need," said Mousebeard. "This ship's not going anywhere...."

The sound of gunfire from the opposite direction caught their attention, and Mousebeard lifted his telescope to the causeway. He saw Indigo, about halfway up the path.

"It's Indigo!" he muttered. "He's running at Battersby...."

Fenwick gazed up at the causeway and the cluster of soldiers, but he couldn't make out anyone in particular. It was just too far away.

"Is Drewshank there? And Emiline? Scratcher?"

Another gunshot echoed through the air.

"What is it?" said Fenwick. "What's happening?"

Mousebeard watched Indigo fall backward through the air and land on his back. He didn't move.

"Indigo's been shot…!"

Fenwick's eyes opened wide.

Mousebeard twisted the telescope a little and focused in on the boy. Battersby approached him and leaned over. Suddenly, Indigo's sword rose and he thrust it into Battersby's leg. The pirate saw the boy attempt to stand. His hand was clutching at his bloody chest, and with one look over the side of the towering stone causeway, he jumped. Mousebeard held his breath. He tried to follow Indigo's passage into the sea, but his movement wasn't fast enough.

"He's jumped into the sea!" said Mousebeard. "He jumped…"

Fenwick jumped back onto land to find more injured sailors.

"And where's Algernon when we need him?" he shouted angrily. "Where is he?"

⇒ ✳ ⇐

When Algernon's eyes opened, he could see the blue sky above him. There was a repeated clanking noise emanating from his head, which he initially thought was a headache, but when he moved his body, he realized it was his suit washing against some rocks with the swell of the sea. The suit was floating with the aid of four small airbags that had inflated around its midriff, and he tried to level it so that he was upright. It wasn't an easy task, and he ended up using one of the robotic claws to attach it to a rock. Once he'd done this he found that he did, in fact, have a blinding headache.

Algernon released a small valve, and the helmet loosened, allowing him to twist it off before casting it aside into the sea. He realized that he was at the base of the outcrop when a small rockfall brought him to his senses. Boulders splashed on either side of him, and he suddenly saw the *Stonebreaker* sailing past in his peripheral vision. He squeezed through his suit and immediately felt the icy water chill every inch of him as he began swimming.

It was hard work pushing through the water, fighting the waves and the force of the current, but Algernon soon reached the *Silver Shark*, and with a few more strokes he had swum past. He navigated around its hull and came to the slope of the outcrop as it led up to the causeway. It was the easiest way up onto dry land, but before he'd made his first step up, he saw blood all over his hand. He wiped it clean and patted his body, on the lookout for wounds, but there were none. And then he saw the body floating next to the rocks.

It was lying faceup, and a blossoming cloud of blood was spilling from its chest. Only when he saw the dark hair splayed out around its head did he realize it was Indigo.

"Oh no! No! No! No!" he muttered, and gripped one of the smaller rocks in order to reach out and grab him. His fingers caught hold of Indigo's shirt and reeled him in, oblivious to the weight. Algernon felt a pulse and found there was still a faint heartbeat.

"If we get you through this, my boy," said Algernon, "then I will be a true genius."

> ✻ ⋘

Battersby clenched his leg. The sword had thrust right through, leaving a clean wound, and he sat patiently while a soldier bandaged it tight.

"Locarno, get your men to jump that gap," he ordered. "I want Mousebeard and I don't care what it takes!"

The soldier sent out the order, and within a few seconds the troops were leaping across the severed path.

"They're coming for us!" shouted Fenwick. "Hurry up!"

The last of the remaining sailors rushed aboard ship, and just as Fenwick set about sealing the armored gangplanks, he heard Algernon's voice.

"Fenwick! Anyone!" he shouted, as he stumbled onto the causeway.

"Is that Algernon?" said Mousebeard.

"And he's got Indigo!" cried Fenwick. He ran onto the ground and rushed to the bow of the ship.

Algernon had never looked so happy.

"Take him," he said, "or else I just might die."

Fenwick pulled Indigo onto his shoulder. He could see the Guard running at them, and gunshots fired from behind him.

"Get in here!" shouted Mousebeard from the edge of the ship, pistols smoking from both his hands. "What are you waiting for?"

They ran around and leapt onto the deck as the Old Town Guard continued firing at them. Bullets chimed against the *Silver Shark*'s hull, but nothing could penetrate it once the armored sides had been sealed.

# The Bearded Mouse

A WIDE-EYED MOUSE THAT IS POPULAR WITH COLLECTORS, THE BEARDED *Mouse has a tufty growth of hair under its chin that gives it the appearance of having a beard. In the wild, this creature lives in small groups (or communes, as collectors fondly call them), and the alpha mouse is always the one with the longest beard. Only the males of the species have this extra growth of hair, so it is easy to discern between sexes for breeding.*

## MOUSING NOTES

*These mice must be kept in groups, but their cheerful and relaxed disposition makes them a pleasure to own. Their diet consists solely of vegetables and seeds, so they are an inexpensive addition to any collection.*

# The Curse

THE SILVER SHARK WAS UNDER SIEGE. THE STONEBREAKER had destroyed any defenses that the outcrop had given to Mousebeard, and its guns were now focusing solely on his ship. Water had breached the hull once more and was seeping through the rivets, its flow growing stronger by the second. Sailors did their best to clog up any of the ship's open wounds, but they were fighting a losing battle.

On the gun deck a table had been dragged into the open space between the cannons, and Indigo was hauled onto its surface. He was in a bad way; the wound on his chest was bleeding profusely and his shirt was now totally red.

"Do what you can for him, Algernon," said Mousebeard,

overlooking the guns. They were running low on cannon-balls, and any piece of metal — cutlery, chains, jewelry, anything they could find — had been piled up for use.

"I don't expect him to see the night through," said Algernon, "but I'll try my best."

He took hold of the boy's shirt and tore it open to get a better look at the wound. Algernon's face paled. The wound was dark and messy and scattered with shot, but that was the least of his worries. Winding fully around Indigo's arm, etched in the finest detail, was a black tattoo consisting of spirals and circles. Algernon immediately recognized it.

"Jonathan…," he said quietly.

"Not now…"

Algernon insisted. He grabbed Mousebeard's arm as he attempted to walk by.

"Jonathan, you have to see this.…"

Mousebeard was taken aback by Algernon's actions. He looked across in disgust, but then his disgust changed to horror. The tattoo on Indigo's arm was a sign of the boy's allegiance — it was a sign of his homeland.

"He's Illyrian...," said Mousebeard.

"A member of their royalty, no less. They are the only ones who get to wear the crest around their arm."

"Blast him!" said Mousebeard. "You think he was spying on us?"

"I think his intentions may have been bad, yes."

"But I saw him attack Battersby! I don't get it!"

Algernon placed his hands at either side of Indigo's chest. He stared at the wound, as if wishing it to heal itself.

"Perhaps he knew that we weren't his enemy — the Illyrians, after all, are not aggressive types by nature."

"I read that the Illyrians had unleashed Death Squads — we were being hunted down whether we knew it or not."

"Surely not!" exclaimed Algernon. He looked at Indigo and wished that the boy's life didn't rest in his hands.

"Do what you can to save him, Algernon. Do it...!"

Mousebeard walked away, fuming.

"We'll only find out the truth if he stays alive," he said, before climbing up to the top deck.

Algernon was left to decide Indigo's fate. It wasn't a

position he liked. He brushed the hair from the boy's face and remembered that, above all, everyone deserved the benefit of the doubt. He picked up his tools and began removing the gunshot that littered the weeping wound.

≫ ✳ ≪

Mousebeard slunk around the top deck. He could hear the Old Town Guard on the causeway, readying themselves for something, and he clenched his pistols as tightly as his hands were able.

"I hate this," said Fenwick. "Where's Mr. Drewshank? I know he'd never have let them attack us. Something must have happened...."

"We've got enough to worry about as it is," said Mousebeard. "Let's line our deck with cannons—our best defense is attack. We can't avoid it now, so let's give it to them."

Fenwick enjoyed the defiance in the pirate's voice. He recognized something of Drewshank in him. He called all the soldiers that weren't on the gun deck to join him and help prepare the ship for their last stand.

"So then, Battersby," shouted Mousebeard. "What are you threatening me with this time?"

The shadow that had spread over the *Silver Shark* deepened. Dusk was approaching. On the causeway, the Old Town Guard had formed an unbreakable line of rifles; all were aimed at the armored gangplanks that rose above their heads, giving them no view of those on deck.

"I'm not threatening you with anything," Battersby replied, pacing back and forth behind his artillery. "As you can tell, I've called off the *Stonebreaker*'s attack. Now all I ask is for you to capitulate—you know, wave the white flag, surrender…"

"You want me to do all the hard work for you?" boomed Mousebeard. "If you want me, you'll have to come and get me."

"Break down the defenses," Battersby ordered his troops.

The soldiers threw grappling hooks over the ship's side and started to pull. The metal sheeting over the hull creaked and clunked as it was pulled apart.

"It's only a matter of time," said Fenwick to the pirate beside him.

The cannons were lined up in wait, with the sailors behind.

"Hold up your weapons, men," said Mousebeard through gritted teeth. "Once the sides fall, we strike."

⇒ ✳ ⇐

Emiline crawled through the square tunnel on her hands and knees. All around her was the glow of Methuselah Mice, and no longer were there just the few who'd entered the tomb. Hundreds of mice had emerged from holes in the walls of earth as they'd progressed, and each one was following them.

"These robes make life hard, don't they!" said Drewshank, who was finding the cramped conditions the most bothersome. "Not only do they not match my shoes, but they weigh a ton!"

"If it stops them from attacking us, we shouldn't complain," said Scratcher.

"Hmmm, maybe," he grumbled in reply. "They smell horrible too...."

When Emiline had taken a Mouse Warrior's suit for herself, she realized that there was a metal grille on the side of the mask that could be opened. Once they'd all slid them across, it became much easier to hear one another.

"Wait a second!" said Emiline, surprising Drewshank and Scratcher by standing up a little way in front. "It's the exit…or was…."

She found herself in a brick-lined chamber, its roof a mess of tree roots. She lifted her hands and used the long claws of the Warrior suit to cut through some of them. Great clumps of earth crumbled and dropped from above as she poked around, and suddenly a pile of thick stone slabs careered to the ground. She ducked and threw her hands over her head, and without warning the bright blue glow of the mice became stronger. Once the subsidence had slowed to a trickle of dirt, the glow died down once more.

"It's as though we have guardian angels," she said, looking above her. She was so happy to see the sky.

Scratcher crawled into the chamber and saw the natural light above them, and a terrific sense of relief washed over him.

"It really is the way out…," he said.

"Come on, then!" exclaimed Drewshank, pushing himself into the space around his fellow Mouse Warriors—gnarled roots were touching the spines rising from the top of his mask. "Let's get out of here!"

They clambered out one after another, trying to avoid the hundreds of Methuselah Mice that were following their every step. As they emerged they all realized they were in the ruins where they'd spent the night. It looked to be in an even worse state now that half of the remaining floor had fallen in, but the best news was that they were so near the gate — and so close to their friends on the *Silver Shark*.

Drewshank led the way and was soon comfortable in his outfit. He felt strangely powerful in the ancient clothes, and he knew for a fact that anyone seeing him for the first time would be scared out of their wits — at least that was how he felt when he looked at Scratcher and Emiline. By the time they reached the steps rising up to the gate, there were too many Methuselah Mice around them to count; the mice appeared to be descending from the trees, crawling out of the ground, and even falling from the sky. And all of them had taken on the glow of the others. The unearthly light that they gave out was as beautiful as it was frightening to Emiline, especially as she knew its real power.

The three Warriors started the uneven climb to the gate and made their way through.

⇒ ✳ ⇐

Piece after piece of the metal hull warped and buckled under the strain of the Old Town Guard's grappling hooks, and Mousebeard looked across at a sailor with the intention of making him unlock the sides. He was wondering how long they could last before attacking, when the mouse in his beard scratched his chin. He pried the thick hair apart and tried to stroke it, but the mouse was unsettled, and its paws kicked out again nervously. He closed up his beard and thought no more of it when a faint blue glow spread in front of his eyes.

"Your beard...," said Fenwick. He was staring at the pirate's face as though he'd seen a ghost.

Mousebeard stepped backward and the glow followed him. His thoughts flew back to the old lady on Stormcloud Island and that moment when he collapsed. He remembered her face and the Methuselah Mouse beside her.

Suddenly, the pull of the hooks slackened, and the

awful noise of twisting metal ceased. Mousebeard glanced at Fenwick. Across the sky, the dull evening light was turning to night, but surrounding the path winding up to Norgammon was a bright blue light, the same as that which radiated from his beard.

"Unlock the gangplanks," ordered Mousebeard.

The sailor holding the locks looked uncertain. He didn't move his hand.

"Do it," barked Mousebeard.

The *Silver Shark*'s armored side clattered down onto the sharp rocks, and they saw for themselves the sight that had stopped Battersby's troops dead in their tracks. The three Mouse Warriors, their bodies humming with the glow of the Methuselah Mice, were standing a short way up the causeway. Thousands of mice surrounded them, their trail of blue light leading all the way back to the gate.

"Who are you?" said Battersby. He marched up the path, pistol in hand. Locarno stayed with the other troops and held his rifle targeted at the pirate. The Mouse Warriors didn't reply.

"I order you to reveal yourselves!"

When they failed to reply for a second time, Battersby took offense. He lifted his gun and pointed it at the closest of the three, which was also the tallest.

"If you fail to answer me, I will shoot you," he said. "I am not afraid...."

Drewshank finally spoke out.

"But you should be afraid," he said.

"I know that voice," said Battersby. "Devlin Drews..."

Before he finished his words, he pulled the trigger of his gun. Drewshank flew backward with the force of the blast and landed in a heap. The armor around his chest had protected him, but he felt as if a heavyweight fighter had hit him square in the ribs. He coughed and pushed his clawed hand against the stone path.

"You didn't want to do that...," he said, choking slightly.

The Methuselah Mice crept forward, their eyes glowing a bright blue and the air around them fizzing with electricity. Their glow grew stronger and stronger, the light forming an arc of blue in the sky that could be seen for miles. As Battersby reloaded his weapon, the mice attacked.

"No!" cried Mousebeard. His beard erupted into a mass of bright blue sparks that connected with all the other mice on the causeway. He felt his chest tighten and his thoughts weaken. His breathing became strained, and he fell against Fenwick as his legs gave way. Fenwick grabbed him and was just about able to control his fall as the light consumed everyone.

Battersby watched the blue light descend on him like lightning leaping between sky and ground. He tried to brush it off as though it was a swarm of flies, but he could do nothing to stop its deadly intention. He felt his legs grow tense, and his hands rolled into fists—his fingernails cutting into his palms. He saw his shoulders and chest ripple with electricity as they contorted, bending unnaturally. His legs were now twisting inward, cracking noises piercing the air as their bones splintered. It was as though something was attacking him from the inside: his insides were boiling, growing hotter and hotter, and his skin started to tighten around his flesh, constricting his movements. His every limb began to shake as the noise in his ears tore into his mind. He saw his soldiers fearfully falling to the ground, their faces petrified. Eventually, as the pain surging through his body grew unbearable, he let out a bloodcurdling scream and collapsed on the floor.

⋙ ✳ ⋘

"Mousebeard!" said Drewshank, kneeling on the deck of the *Silver Shark*. He tapped the pirate's cheeks lightly and was cheered by the rosy glow forming on Mousebeard's chin. Emiline was sitting next to him, with Portly in her hands. The mouse was squeaking loudly.

Mousebeard stirred—his eyes blinking slowly before opening wide.

"How do you feel?" asked Drewshank.

"My ears are ringing," he replied. "And my chest aches...."

"He's all right!" shouted Drewshank, putting an end to everyone's fears.

Mousebeard coughed.

"But you have a mousehead?" he said.

"Ah, yes..."

Drewshank removed the mask and sat it next to the pair of clawed gloves. Emiline did the same.

"The Methuselah Mouse!" exclaimed Mousebeard, trying to sit up. "It was the mouse!"

He felt his beard, but it was empty.

"It ran away," said Fenwick.

"And I doubt you'd find it amongst that bunch out there," added Emiline.

"All along, it was the blasted mouse!"

Mousebeard could see the light glowing from the outcrop. Locarno hadn't dared run to Battersby's rescue. He'd told his soldiers to lower their guns and surrender, and they were sitting surrounded by an uncountable number of Methuselah Mice. The soldiers didn't move, as Scratcher was in charge, still dressed in the clothes of a Warrior, and wherever he moved, the mice followed.

"But the curse...," said Mousebeard. "If that mouse cursed me..."

The pirate gripped Drewshank's shoulder and tried to stand. He had a feeling of emptiness inside him—a feeling of freedom. Something had changed. He pulled himself to his feet.

"And Battersby?" he muttered, staggering forward. "Where is he?"

"Battersby's dead," said Drewshank. "He got what was coming to him. I hadn't expected him to die so horrifically, but he deserved it. There's not much left of him to see...."

"Good, the last thing I'd want to do is see him again."

"We have prisoners, though. It would appear that the *Stonebreaker* is ours for the taking!"

"That could be helpful....Have you seen the *Silver Shark* lately?" grumbled Mousebeard. "She'll be lucky to leave this place!"

Mousebeard inhaled the fresh sea air so that it filled his lungs, and he came to a halt at the edge of his ship. He looked at the rocks and cobblestones that formed the surface of the causeway and then, lifting his right boot warily, leapt across. Despite making the distance, he crashed to the ground, landing on his palms and knees after his weakened legs failed him. But he didn't scream out in pain. His body wasn't tightening and dying inside.

Emiline jumped across and slid to the ground beside him. She pulled back his mass of hair and found that he was smiling.

"Mousebeard?" she said. Portly crawled from her hand and sniffed the pirate's nose.

He stretched out and stroked the mouse.

"I can breathe," he said. "I can touch the ground...."

Emiline leaned closer and shoved her arm under Mousebeard's shoulder. With a great push she helped him clamber to his feet, and Portly, being the mouse that always had to be involved in everything, scurried up his leg and over his jacket and came to rest on his shoulder.

"Your curse?" she said.

Mousebeard's face was a picture of serenity. It looked as though he'd shed ten years over the course of the past few minutes.

"It's gone," he said, staring at the ground under his feet. He wanted to scream. He wanted to cry. He wanted to fall back down to the ground and kiss it.

"It's gone...."

Emiline heard Algernon's voice from the deck.

"Jonathan?" he said excitedly, as he appeared at the side of the ship. His face lit up at the sight of his old friend standing on solid ground.

"You're..."

"I am!" replied Mousebeard.

Algernon jumped to the ground and stared at him from head to toe.

"Well I never…"

"It was the Methuselah Mouse," said Mousebeard. "They seem to harbor some magical power that not even we could have known about."

"And you had it in your beard all this time?"

"All this time…"

"And Indigo?" said Mousebeard, his tone darkening.

"Indigo?" said Emiline.

"He'll survive. But for how long depends on you."

"What? Where is he?" asked Emiline, struggling to have her voice heard.

Drewshank had been listening to their conversation, and he stepped over to join them.

"What's happened?" he asked seriously.

"Indigo is no friend of ours," said Mousebeard. "He's an assassin."

Emiline felt as though the world had broken apart beneath her, and she was falling down with no means of stopping.

# The Flycatcher Mouse

THE FLYCATCHER MOUSE IS ONE OF THE SMALLEST SPECIES OF MOUSE AND
lives off insects and berries. Its method for catching prey is very unusual in the mouse
kingdom because it utilizes its exceptionally long, sticky tongue. This can be extended
to almost a meter in length and reaches speeds of 150 meters per hour prior to hitting
and stunning its target.

Emanating from the jungles of Western Promethia, the Flycatcher Mouse is very
popular with collectors.

MOUSING NOTES

This is a tropical mouse and so needs a cage with water features and high humidity.

# Indigo

FEELING SORE?" SAID ALGERNON, PULLING THE BANDAGES tighter over Indigo's chest and securing them with a pin.

They were sitting in Mousebeard's cabin, while most of the sailors were busy tending to the ship's battle wounds. Indigo opened his eyes and saw Mousebeard and Drewshank at his side. Algernon poured a cup of water and held it close to his lips.

"How do you feel?" asked Mousebeard.

Indigo breathed deeply; pain shot through his body as his chest rose.

"Alive," he said, his mouth dry. He drew in a little water from the cup and swallowed it down.

"So when did you plan to tell us?" said Mousebeard.

"What?" he said defensively.

"Your secret's out," said Drewshank.

"My secret?"

Mousebeard grabbed his shoulder, and Indigo yelled out.

"So you don't understand words, but you understand pain?" said the pirate, loosening his grip.

Indigo's eyes darkened.

"You're lucky," said Drewshank. "Algernon thought enough of you to give you the chance to explain yourself. He cleaned your wound and certainly saved your life."

"So it would seem," he said, his words slow and painful. "Thank you...."

Emiline ran into the cabin and shouted at Drewshank.

"What are you doing?" she screamed. "Leave him alone!"

"Emiline!" said Algernon firmly. "For once this doesn't concern you."

"Of course it concerns me," she said. "You're all as bad as Lord Battersby!"

"Get out!" shouted Mousebeard. His words hit Emiline hard. She thought she was used to him by now, but his voice shook her to the core.

Emiline shrank to the back of the cabin. She felt tiny and insignificant, but she was determined not to leave.

"I didn't mean to fool you," said Indigo. He stretched his arm out and took the cup from Algernon's hand to drink some more.

"I don't believe you," said Mousebeard. "You had every intention of deceiving us."

Indigo took another gulp of water. The pain in his chest consumed him.

"The only way we can ever trust you is for you to be truthful now," said Drewshank.

"I never lied to you," Indigo said, his eyes staring hard into Drewshank's.

Mousebeard was in a fearsome mood. He clenched his fist and slammed it into the hard chair that Indigo was resting in.

"You have always been a liar," he shouted. "Just who are you really?"

"That's enough," said Algernon. "He's in no state for this."

"I don't care what state he's in. He once had every intention of killing us all — he's an Illyrian!"

"Stop...," said Indigo. He pulled the blood-soaked hair from his face. "I'm an Illyrian....Yes, I thought you were a danger...."

"And you still do?" snarled Mousebeard.

"You stole the Golden Mice. That makes you an enemy to my country."

"But you saw what was going on in Hamlyn," said Drewshank sternly, "and you think we're the enemy?"

"It is our way!" said Indigo.

"Your way?" said Emiline. She couldn't hold back any longer. "What are you? Who are you?"

"He's an Illyrian spy," said Mousebeard.

"Illyrian *royalty*...," added Algernon.

"Royalty?" said Emiline.

"You know that too?" said Indigo regretfully.

"I know what your tattoos mean," said Mousebeard. "What did you take me for? A fool?"

"Never!" he said, pulling himself upright. "And I know now that your actions were always in the best interests of Illyria. I know that our forces and my father will soon be leaving for Old Town to retrieve the stolen Golden Mice. They don't know the truth yet, but they will."

"And how will they?" said Drewshank. "We're at least three months' sailing from Old Town."

"I'll get word to them...."

"How?" said Algernon. "By mouse? Because I can tell you now that all messages flying in and out of the port are being intercepted."

"Just get me to Old Town, and I'll do the rest."

Emiline was deathly silent. Even she had been fooled.

"I'm sorry," said Indigo. "But I had to find out the truth my own way. I can clear your names. Believe me...."

"You know there's no way we'll be able to land at Old Town," said Drewshank.

"And my submarine's finished," added Algernon. "The *Silver Shark* will in no way last out the journey either."

Mousebeard looked out of the window and saw Battersby's warship. It had dropped anchor at Locarno's request and was waiting for his instructions.

"We could use the *Stonebreaker*...," he said, his temper easing. "There are, after all, a number of scores to settle...."

Drewshank found it hard not to laugh.

"You're not suggesting we return to Old Town in Battersby's ship?" he said. When he said the words aloud, a twinkle came to his eye. Maybe it didn't sound like such a bad idea after all.

"There's no way they could have sent a message home from this distance — nobody would know anything about what's happened here," said Algernon excitedly.

"It almost sounds possible!" said Drewshank.

"And I swear I shall do all I can to clear your names," said Indigo. "Just give me a chance...."

Mousebeard walked to the door and turned to look at the boy.

"You have a lot to prove," he said, "but in this case we have nothing to lose and everything to gain."

"Remember, there are still troops in Norgammon," said Drewshank. "There's even Miserley out there somewhere!"

"They'll come with a little persuasion," said Mousebeard. "The Methuselah Mice will help.... And we need all the prisoners and bargaining power we can get."

"And Isiah?" said Algernon.

Mousebeard's thundering laugh rattled the woodwork.

"Our old friend Isiah Lovelock won't know what's hit him...."

# The Floating Puffer Mouse

NOT AN AQUATIC MOUSE BY NATURE, THE FLOATING PUFFER IS THOUGHT TO take to water simply because it prefers it to its more natural habitat of sand dunes. Gaining its name from its inflatable belly, the Floating Puffer uses a gaseous exchange (from eating an indigestible type of black seaweed) to bloat itself. The mouse can float on its back for days, only having to return to land to eat more seaweed.

It's been said that in the old days, sailors were thought to hear the whispers of doomed maidens when a storm was about to strike—but in fact it's very likely they were hearing the sounds of the Floating Puffer dealing with its problem of self-inflicted wind.

MOUSING NOTES

*This mouse can be kept quite happily in a water tank environment, although you must provide plenty of vegetation. Because of its diet, the Floating Puffer can create quite a stink, so beware!*

# Epilogue

ANY NEWS?" ASKED BEATRICE PETTIFOGGER. SHE WAS sitting in Isiah Lovelock's office, her fingers playing restlessly on the stem of a wineglass. Lovelock was looking out of the window into the dark night. His breath was steaming the windowpane, and he appeared paler than usual.

"I imagine they are out of messenger range, Beatrice. We shall hear from them in time, no doubt."

"You're probably right," she said quietly.

"But this matter with the escaped mice...," he said ominously. "Is Hamlyn secure?"

Pettifogger smarted a little. Indigo's leaving present had

dealt a greater blow to the Trading Center than even he could have imagined.

"Hamlyn is under quarantine," she said. "The Old Town Guard has blocked the port, and no one can leave or enter."

"Good... these violent golden breeds of yours could be our downfall if word gets out."

"I know, I know. But I have it on good authority that the best and most discreet Mousehunter in Midena will arrive soon. We shall have the mice back under observation in no time."

"Make certain it happens....I—"

Lovelock suddenly grasped his chest. His body slumped toward the window, and his face pressed into the glass.

"Isiah?!" shouted Lady Pettifogger, leaping up and rushing to her friend. "What is it? What's wrong?"

Lovelock's legs buckled and he tumbled to the floor. His breathing became forced and his vision was clouding over.

"The curse...," he muttered. "Something's happened....Mousebeard..."

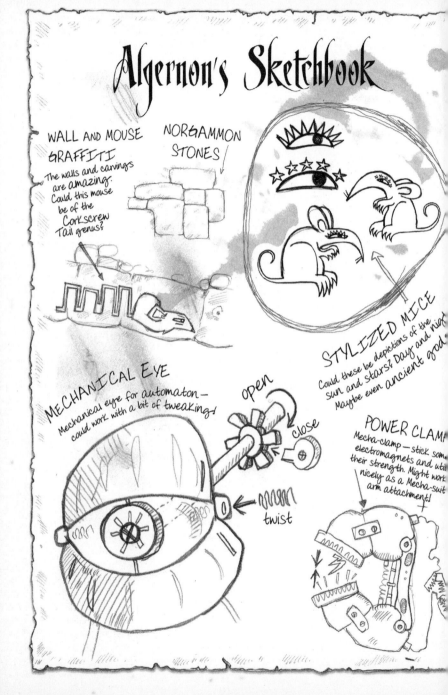

# Algernon's Sketchbook

**WALL AND MOUSE GRAFFITI**
The walls and carvings are amazing. Could this mouse be of the Corkscrew Tail genus?

**NORGAMMON STONES**

**STYLIZED MICE**
Could these be depictions of the sun and stars? Day and night? Maybe even ancient god.

**MECHANICAL EYE**
Mechanical eye for automaton — could work with a bit of tweaking!

open

close

twist

**POWER CLAMP**
Mecha-clamp — stick som electromagnets and util their strength. Might work nicely as a Mecha-suit arm attachment!

wind resistance

Mechanical Wing

spin

Wind Turbines in the MURAL ISLES

MOUSE STATUE  What craftsmanship! And what a size!

Decorated mouse tusk

Mouse carrier

MOUSE WARRIOR

Drewshank looked the part in this amazing Warrior outfit. Of course he would...

TEMPLE

What a sight from afar! I guess they are temples to the **dead** I wish I knew more

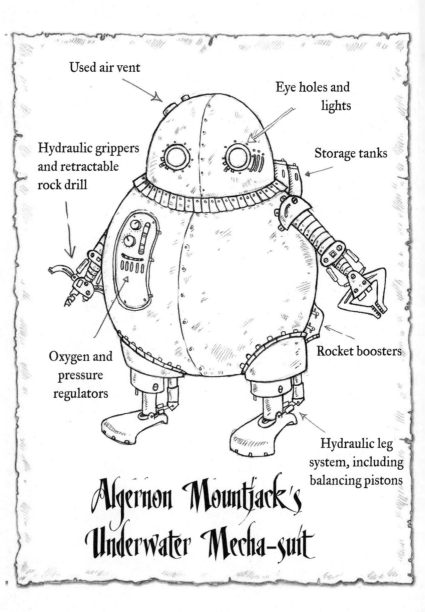

Used air vent

Eye holes and lights

Hydraulic grippers and retractable rock drill

Storage tanks

Oxygen and pressure regulators

Rocket boosters

Hydraulic leg system, including balancing pistons

Algernon Mountjack's
Underwater Mecha-suit

# Mousing Implements

Popo drop canister

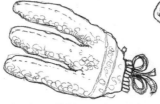

Chainmail Sharpclaw glove

Fur-flint lighter

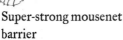

Super-strong mousenet barrier

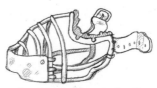

Angry mouse muzzle

Mousenip pouch

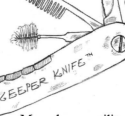

Mousekeeper utility knife [including claw clippers, knife, comb, and ear cleaners]

# Acknowledgments

A FEW PEOPLE HAVE HELPED ME IMMEASURABLY during the making of this book:

*Tom Percival*—thanks for all your support and excellent advice.

*John, Justine, and Willa at The Bookseller Crow*—I couldn't have asked for a better bookshop at the top of my road.

*Fraser Campbell*—what a great idea for a mouse you had!

*Susi Weaser and Laura Smith*—you promised to dress as mice and you didn't let me down!

*Mum, Dad, Gran, Rob, Cindy, Bob, and Jeanette Lee*—thank you for being parents.

*Katie Lee*—not only are you the inventor of exploding mouse poo, but you're also my favorite girl.

*And a special thank-you goes to:*

Brennan Alkin, Oliver and Caroline Battersby, Lia Devlin, John Fenech, the Garners, and Glen Lovelock—without you I'd have had to come up with a load of other names!